HARLEQUIN®
*M*akes any time special ®

ISBN 0-373-18788-2

9 780373 187881

50425

EAN

Susanne McCarthy

HIS PERFECT WIFE

DBV470973

"What about…Eleni?" Megan demanded, her voice as ragged as her breathing.

"Ah, yes… My virgin bride, if Cousin Sophia has her way. I confess the idea has its merits. Not that virgins are particularly to my taste. I tend to like my woman like my wine—a little more mature, with that little extra…something to intrigue the palate."

That lazy fingertip was still circling over her breasts, closer and tantalizingly closer to the ripened peaks that now showed so pertly and invitingly beneath the taut blue Lycra. Part of her hated him for treating her like this, but part of her knew that she only had to tell him to stop and he would. But, to her shame, she didn't want him to stop. She wanted him to go on—though he was stripping away every inch of her self-respect.

SUSANNE McCARTHY grew up in south London, but she always wanted to live in the country, and shortly after her marriage she moved to Shropshire with her husband. She lives in a house on a hill with lots of dogs and cats. She loves to travel—but she loves to come home. As well as her writing, she still enjoys her career as a teacher in adult education, though she works only part-time now.

Susanne McCarthy

HIS PERFECT WIFE

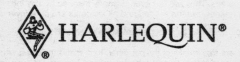

HARLEQUIN®

TORONTO • NEW YORK • LONDON
AMSTERDAM • PARIS • SYDNEY • HAMBURG
STOCKHOLM • ATHENS • TOKYO • MILAN • MADRID
PRAGUE • WARSAW • BUDAPEST • AUCKLAND

ISBN 0-373-18788-2

HIS PERFECT WIFE

First North American Publication 2002.

This edition published by arrangement with Harlequin Books S.A.

® and TM are trademarks of the publisher. Trademarks indicated with
® are registered in the United States Patent and Trademark Office, the
Canadian Trade Marks Office and in other countries.

Visit us at www.eHarlequin.com

Printed in U.S.A.

CHAPTER ONE

'HE'S coming—I've just seen his car!'

'Who's coming?' Megan didn't even bother to glance up from the pile of path-lab returns she was checking. She could guess who had caused such a flutter in the ward sister's ample breast.

'Theo Nikolaides!' Sally Henderson, a happily married mother of two boisterous teenage sons, and most of the time the epitome of efficiency and professionalism, was excitedly checking her lipstick in the tiny mirror sellotaped to the back of the nurses' station. 'Oh, come on—even you've got to admit he's a hunk!'

'Possibly,' Megan conceded, a glint of sardonic humour in her fine grey eyes. 'Unfortunately he knows it, which rather spoils the effect. Anyway, he's all yours,' she added as one of the call-lights began to flash. 'I'm going to empty Mrs Van Doesburgh's bedpan!'

She always preferred to be doing something else when Theo Nikolaides came to visit his father. She had had enough of good-looking, arrogant men to last her a lifetime. Not that she had ever exchanged so much as one word with him—she didn't need to. You could tell just by the way he strode through the cloistered hush of the private ward, his dark head held at an aloof angle, a faintly cynical smile twisting that hard mouth, that he regarded the whole world as his dominion.

It must be in the genes, she mused wryly. Old Theodakis Nikolaides, his father, was a holy terror— even some of the doctors were afraid of him, and he had managed to reduce most of the nurses to tears at one time or another. Though to be honest Megan had a bit of a soft spot for him—she had been a theatre sister in her last job, and she wasn't easily intimidated. And he seemed to like the fact that she stood up to him—more than once she had caught a twinkle in his eye when they had been in the middle of one of their regular confrontations.

To be fair, much of his bad temper was probably due to frustration at the effects of his stroke—apparently he had previously been a very active man, still running the hotel chain he had virtually built from scratch in his native Cyprus, though he had turned seventy. And anyone would be irritated by that family! All those nieces and nephews and cousins, sitting around squabbling over their inheritance as if he were already dead.

At least she couldn't accuse his son of that, she acknowledged fairly. He visited every afternoon without fail—though he usually stayed no more than twenty minutes. And he usually managed to have a flaming row with his father. But afterwards the old man was always in a splendid humour.

She caught a glimpse of the son as she closed the door on Mrs Van Doesburgh's room. She had to concede that Sally was right—he could definitely be described as a hunk. He was several inches over six feet tall, with a pair of wide shoulders that were today, as usual, moulded by a jacket of very expensive black leather, and long, lean legs in soft black denim jeans.

She hadn't ever really seen his face properly, but she had the impression of a high forehead, a straight nose, and a hard jaw. His hair was black, cut very short and sleek against his head. He reminded her of a panther, she mused, watching as he walked past, his long, lazy stride charged with the latent energy of a jungle cat. A natural predator, dark and dangerous...

And best avoided at all costs, she reminded herself crisply. Let Sally make doe eyes at him if she wanted to—for herself, she preferred to stay well out of his way. Besides, she was much too busy to waste time even thinking about Theo Nikolaides. For the next fifteen minutes she was fully occupied in dealing with Mrs Van Doesburgh.

When the agency had sent her to work on a private ward she had been reluctant, believing it would be all spoiled society dames coming in for cosmetic surgery, or irritable old businessmen having heart by-passes that wouldn't have been necessary if they'd taken fewer liquid lunches and more exercise. But she had quickly come to realise that the people here were as sick as anyone, and being rich didn't take away one ounce of their discomfort. She had been here for almost five weeks now, and she was finding it just as challenging, just as rewarding, as her previous job.

She finished attending to Mrs Van Doesburgh. Settling her comfortably for her nap, she then laid a paper towel carefully over the bedpan, and picked it up to take it back to the sluice. But as she opened the door she almost collided with someone striding along the passage, disdainfully indifferent towards lesser mortals.

Her gaze travelled up over the wide cliff of a shoulder, clad in black leather, to meet a pair of the most incredible blue eyes—eyes the colour of lapis lazuli, and all the more startling in contrast to his raven-black hair. Funny, she mused abstractedly—she had assumed that his eyes would be brown, like his father's, though she knew from a half-remembered lecture on genetics that that did not necessarily have to be the case...

At the moment they were glaring down at her in sharp annoyance. 'Shouldn't you look where you're going?' he demanded impatiently.

Her own eyes sparked; the near-accident had been his fault. But it would be unprofessional—and quite pointless—to allow herself to argue with him. So she forced herself to swallow the tart retort that had sprung to her lips. 'Excuse me,' she murmured demurely, stepping past him into the sluice.

He had managed to stay even less time than usual today—yet another quarrel with his father, she surmised wryly. They were too much alike—both proud and stubborn. But it was a pity he couldn't make more of an effort to get along with the old man—he was his only child, after all, and though he would never have admitted it Dakis doted on him. He was always talking about him.

Theo's mother had been English. Dakis had never told Megan what had gone wrong, but the marriage had ended when Theo was twelve years old, and she had taken him back to England. Six months later she had been killed in a car accident, but Theo had refused to return home to live with his father, preferring to stay with an uncle.

And, even since he had grown up, he had refused repeated pleas by his father to take a role in the family business, choosing instead to strike out on his own. He had started off with a few hundred pounds of borrowed capital, publishing a free entertainments review magazine that had been given out on street corners all over London. It had quickly gained cult status, with advertisers virtually throwing money at him—it had made him a millionaire in less than two years.

Now he seemed to dabble in a little bit of everything—restaurants, record shops, theatre productions. In his more irascible moods, Dakis had castigated him as a playboy. 'Always got some flighty piece on his arm,' he had grumbled. 'A different one every time I see him. Oh, he's got taste, I'll give him that. But they're not the sort I'd want to be the mother of my grandson.'

He was unlikely to have much success in persuading his son to change his lifestyle, Megan mused with a touch of amusement. Why would he? Theo seemed to have everything a man could want—plenty of money, and plenty of beautiful women to spend it on. The kind of women who could spend three hours having a manicure, who would have no idea what it was like to work a ten-hour shift on a busy hospital ward with no lunch break and barely even time to sit down. Ah, well, maybe one day she would win the National Lottery—if she ever had time to buy a ticket!

She frowned slightly as she caught a glimpse of her own reflection in the shining steel of the sluice cabinet. It wasn't an image that usually caused her to frown. Though she wasn't in the same league as Theo Nikolaides' women, she would generally regard herself as reasonably good-looking. But not at the moment.

It was the hair. She should have known better than to let her sister anywhere near it! Just highlights, Cathy had promised—nothing too drastic. Just something to give her a lift, after the trauma of breaking off her engagement to Jeremy. It had come out yellow.

Her first instinct had been to rush out and buy a bottle of dye to take it back to its natural honey-brown, but Cathy had warned her that that could make it turn green. She had had it cut to a jaw-length bob that she could keep neatly tucked up under her cap for work, hiding the dark roots that were already showing through, but short of opting for a Kojak cut she was stuck with it for the time being. Well, it was certainly a new image, she thought with a touch of humour—her no-longer-to-be-mother-in-law would have a very refined upper-middle-class fit if she could see it.

Having checked that the small room was clean and tidy, Megan was about to go back to the ward when she realised that one of her suspenders had worked itself undone. She always wore silk stockings rather than tights for work. It was a habit she had adopted in her previous job—the heat in an operating theatre, and the static from all the electrical equipment, could make tights uncomfortable.

It could be thought something of an extravagance, buying silk stockings on a nurse's salary, but she had found they lasted so much better that they were actually more economical. Besides, she liked the feel of them against her skin. Propping her foot up on a carton of paper towels, she lifted the hem of her bottle-green uniform and carefully smoothed the silk up all the way from her ankle to her thigh, bending her head in concentration as she adjusted the recalcitrant suspender...

A strange prickling sensation at the back of her neck told her that she was being watched. Slowly she turned her head. Theo Nikolaides was standing in the doorway, one wide shoulder leaning lazily against the frame. Those deep blue eyes surveyed the slender length of her legs, before lifting to meet her gaze with mocking contempt.

A rush of hot scarlet coloured her cheeks, and she quickly brushed down her skirt, turning to confront him. She wasn't quite sure that she could trust her voice, so contented herself with arching one fine eyebrow in what she hoped was a cool enquiry.

'Miss Taylor?'

'*Nurse* Taylor,' she corrected him with brittle dignity.

That hard mouth curved into a sardonic smile. 'My father tells me you're his favourite nurse,' he remarked on a note of dry disdain.

'Oh?'

'He didn't tell me why.'

She shrugged her slender shoulders. 'Does there need to be a particular reason?'

'Probably not—not in my father's case.' He let that insolent blue gaze slide down over her again in a cool appraisal, from the brassy bottle-blonde curls crammed up beneath her cap to her slender ankles sheathed in the shimmer of black silk, taking in every curve of her slender body along the way. 'Nothing beyond the obvious, at least.'

His meaning was unmistakable, and her eyes flashed him a frosty warning. But, before she could utter the sharp retort that had sprung to her lips, the soft peep of one of the call-bells began to sound, summoning her away. 'If you'll excuse me?' she requested tautly. 'I'm afraid I am rather busy at the moment, as you can see.'

He stood aside, that cold smile a portent of danger. 'Of course. I wouldn't wish to keep the ministering angel from tending to the sick, now, would I?'

He deliberately left her barely enough room to get past, and she had to brush against him as she stepped through the door. She tried not to let herself be aware of that lean, hard male body, but she couldn't prevent the little shiver of heat that ran through her. He sensed her reaction, and she heard him laugh softly, but she tilted up her head at a proud angle and walked away.

It was fortunate that Mrs Van Doesburgh only needed to have her pillows adjusted this time—Megan was conscious that her hands were still shaking slightly from the encounter. Stupid, she castigated herself roundly—she shouldn't have let him needle her like that. After all, she ought to know everything there was to know about handling arrogant men—she had almost married one.

Dr Jeremy Cramer. The most eligible young doctor at St Mark's, handsome, wealthy, oozing charm, already a registrar, and certain to be a famous orthopaedic surgeon like his father within a few years, exactly as he had planned. Everyone had said she was a very lucky girl to have caught him. The trouble was, he had thought so too.

It had taken a lot of courage to call the whole thing off, with just a few weeks to go to the wedding. Everything had been prepared—the dress made, the flowers ordered, almost two hundred invitations sent out. The presents had even started to arrive. But, as the pressure had built up, she had been forced to recognise that the doubts she had been feeling for some time were a good deal more than pre-wedding nerves.

He hadn't taken it well—but then how could she have expected him to? He had been furious. But the things he had said, even allowing for the fact that it had been in the heat of the moment, had convinced her that she had done the right thing. How could she ever have been happy, married to a man who thought she should be grateful for having been elevated so far above her class? The daughter of a postman marrying a Cramer!

It had been extremely awkward afterwards, still seeing him virtually every day in Theatre. In the end she had felt she had no alternative but to give in her notice. Fortunately for any twinge of conscience she might have felt about jilting him, she had heard soon afterwards on the inter-hospital grapevine that he had already found consolation in the arms of a pretty young trainee pharmacist.

It had seemed like a good idea at the time to come down to London to stay with her little sister Cathy for a while—though perhaps 'little' was no longer a suitable epithet for someone who made a living running up outrageous costumes for rock stars and stand-up comedians, and playing saxophone in an all-girl band!

Unfortunately, much as they loved each other, their lifestyles weren't exactly compatible—except when Megan was working a night-shift, and they could both sleep until lunchtime. But she couldn't afford to get a place of her own. Most of her savings had gone into the house she and Jeremy had been buying together, and though he had rather grudgingly agreed to pay her back her share of the deposit she couldn't expect to recoup anything of the solicitor's fees and all the other incidental costs that had mounted up so alarmingly.

And then there had been the cost of the wedding preparations. Cathy had thought Megan was mad to have insisted on repaying Jeremy's parents every penny of the money they had spent, and perhaps she had been right—the lavish scale of the whole thing had been their idea, not what she had wanted, and they could more than afford it. But her pride wouldn't let her ignore it.

So here she was, free and single—with an overdraft that gave her nightmares, and enough rude letters from the bank manager to paper the living room. She hadn't expected to be able to walk into another theatre sister's job overnight, so she had signed on with the agency while she waited for something suitable to turn up. It was quite a drop in salary, of course, as well as status, but at least she could afford to eat...

Another alarm began to beep, and she shook her head

wryly. If there was one good thing about nursing, it was that it gave you very little time to reflect on your own problems—there were always about a hundred urgent things to do.

Spring was late getting started this year. The bus shelter had been vandalised, so there was no protection from the rain as Megan waited for the bus. Her car had refused to start again this morning, and she wasn't sure when she was going to be able to afford to get it repaired. She hunched into the collar of her raincoat, her hands thrust deep into her pockets. Dakis had told her that the temperature in Cyprus today had been in the middle seventies—it sounded like paradise!

The traffic had slowed for the lights at the corner, so at first she didn't take much notice of the sleek dark blue two-seater that pulled up beside her, until the door opened and a curt voice ordered, 'Get in.'

She wasn't in the habit of responding to that sort of arrogant command, and nor was she in the habit of accepting lifts from virtual strangers. But though the traffic lights had turned to green he was showing no inclination to move on, causing several of the cars behind to beep their horns impatiently, and all the people in the queue to turn and stare. Besides, her wet raincoat would make a lovely mess of his hand-stitched leather seats, she mused with grim pleasure.

The car surged forward as soon as she was in it, not even giving her time to close the door or fasten her seat belt. She struggled to pull herself upright, refusing to give him the satisfaction of a protest. Somehow she managed to sort herself out and recover some semblance of composure, slanting him a fierce glare from beneath her lashes.

He drove without speaking, his profile hard in the yellow glow of the streetlights. With a small sigh of exasperation, Megan sat back, letting herself revel in the warmth and comfort of the car, and listen to the soft, lazy jazz clarinet that was playing on the CD beneath the burr-walnut dashboard.

But after a while she became impatient. 'Thank you for the lift.'

The edge of sarcasm in her voice caused one dark eyebrow to flicker just a fraction. 'It wasn't for your convenience, Miss Taylor—it was for mine.'

'Nurse Taylor,' she reminded him tartly.

'Ah, yes—*Nurse* Taylor,' he conceded. 'You are actually a qualified nurse?'

'Of course.'

'When and where did you qualify?'

'I don't have to answer that,' she retorted hotly. 'I'm employed by the hospital, and they check my qualifications.'

Those incredible lapis lazuli-blue eyes slid towards her, glittering like ice. 'Actually that's not quite true, is it?' he pointed out. 'You're employed by an agency.'

She dismissed the minor quibble with a casual shrug of her shoulders. 'It makes no difference. It's a very reputable agency.'

'So I should hope. How old are you, Miss...*Nurse* Taylor?'

'I don't see that my age is any concern of yours.'

Those eyes slid over her again, coolly appraising. 'You can't be much above twenty-four or -five.'

She laughed with acid humour. 'I'm very flattered. Actually I'm twenty-nine.'

'Really?' He smiled in mocking satisfaction at having

tricked the answer out of her. 'Do you know how old my father is?'

'I've read his case notes,' she returned with frosty dignity, unsure of the direction this conversation was taking. 'He's seventy-two.'

'Almost seventy-three. A gap of more than forty years.'

'Goodness, a mathematical genius!'

'You have a very sharp tongue, Miss Taylor. You should be careful you don't cut yourself with it.'

'Well, if I do, I work in the right place to get myself stitched up,' she quipped facetiously.

'And I would suggest that if you wish to continue to work there you should be a little more…circumspect,' he responded, his voice soft with menace. 'I don't think either the hospital or your agency would look very favourably on your relationship with one of your patients. Particularly one easily old enough to be your grandfather.'

She stared at him, shocked and infuriated. 'You seem to be labouring under some kind of misapprehension, Mr Nikolaides,' she informed him, her jaw taut. 'My relationship with your father is purely professional.'

'Oh, I'm sure it is.' He spared her a single glance that made her quickly check that her skirt hadn't ridden up too high above her knees. 'The question is, which profession?'

She drew in a sharp breath, struggling to control the explosion of anger that was surging up inside her. 'You can drop me here,' she instructed, icily polite. 'I'll walk the rest of the way.'

'I'll take you to your door.'

'Please don't bother,' she snapped.

Those blue eyes glittered. 'Afraid of me?'

'Of course not.'

'You should be,' he murmured, smiling poisonously. 'I can be very dangerous.'

'Very melodramatic,' she countered with a bite of sarcasm. 'But somewhat out of place on the Whitechapel Road.' There was someone waiting at a crossing, and he was forced to stop. Megan seized her moment, unfastening her seat belt and slipping out of the car before he could do anything to prevent her.

'Ugh—morning! Who invented mornings?'

Megan glanced up with a smile as her sister wandered into the kitchen, her magenta-streaked hair sticking out in all directions, the Thai-silk kimono she wore as a dressing gown trailing on the floor. 'You're up early,' she remarked.

Cathy shook her head. 'I haven't been to bed yet. Is that coffee? Is there any more?'

'There is—but if you're going to bed won't it keep you awake?'

Cathy yawned. 'Nothing could keep me awake right now. Are you working today?'

'Yes. In fact I'd better be off—I'm going to have to catch the bus again.'

'Car still playing up?' Cathy queried with casual sympathy. 'Listen, love, do you think you could get the shopping on your way home? I know it's my turn, but I promised to get that silver jacket finished for Luther by tonight—they've got a gig in Croydon. I'll do it next week, I promise.'

Megan made herself bite back the impatient response that sprang to her lips. It was the third time in a month that she had done the shopping when it was Cathy's turn, and it meant getting off the bus two stops early and walking home with half a dozen plastic carrier bags. But Cathy had helped her out when she'd been homeless, and she knew she wasn't charging her the full rent.

'No problem,' she responded with a cheerful smile. She swung her handbag over her shoulder, checking that she had her door key. 'Cheerio, then—see you tonight.'

'Uh-huh,' Cathy responded with another wide yawn. 'Don't work too hard.'

Megan smiled wryly as she waited for the lift. Much as she loved her sister, she wasn't sure how long she would be able to go on living with a bathroom permanently littered with discarded clothing and soggy bits of cotton wool, or a kitchen that worked on the principle of the Mad Hatter's tea party, where things were only washed up when they needed to be used again.

But, to be fair, it wasn't entirely Cathy's fault that Megan wasn't quite feeling her usual merry self today. She hadn't slept very well last night—though she would have preferred not to let herself dwell on the memory of the disturbing dreams that had left her feeling wrung out when the alarm clock had sounded. For once, she had found it extremely difficult to get out of bed, and now if she wasn't lucky enough to catch a bus very quickly she was going to be late for work.

And it was raining again. Oh, well, at least it was Saturday, so the buses might not be too full. There had to be *something* positive to improve the day!

But there was no guarantee of that, as she discovered when she arrived on the ward, almost fifteen minutes late. The place was in uproar; Sally was seething, and another nurse was in tears. From the bellows of anger issuing from the corner suite, she could guess the source of the trouble. Dakis was swearing fluently in Greek and

English. 'Stupid girl. If you worked for me, I would fire you on the spot!'

'What's going on?' she queried, tucking her handbag into her locker.

'Diane tried to take his blood test, but she was having trouble finding the vein,' the ward sister explained in the voice of one whose patience was strained to its outer limit. 'He went ballistic—chucked his water-jug at her. Can you have a go? You seem to have a way with him.'

Megan laughed with dry humour. 'All right—I'll try. We wouldn't happen to have a tranquilliser dart in the drugs cupboard, would we?'

She took the sterile tray and syringe from Diane, and went to fetch a fresh hypodermic needle from the Clean Room, and then, squaring her shoulders, she marched into Dakis Nikolaides' suite.

She was met by a furious glare from eyes that were still demon-bright, though set in a face that was slightly distorted from the effects of his stroke. 'And where have you been?' the old man demanded belligerently.

'I've only just come on duty,' she responded calmly. 'I do like to go home now and then, you know. And there's no need for you to be so rude to people.'

'Well, they get my back up,' he grumbled, plucking impatiently at the bed-sheet. 'Toadying. Everyone toadies to me.'

'Of course they do,' she responded briskly, putting the sterile tray down on the bedside table, and going to fetch a couple of paper towels to mop up the spilled water from the floor. 'They're scared of you.'

'Are you saying I'm a bully?' he demanded, bristling.

'What do you think?'

'Well, you're not scared of me.'

'No, I'm not,' she retorted. 'So just calm down, and let me take your blood test.'

'Oh, all right,' he conceded grudgingly, holding out his arm. 'Stick me full of holes if you must. You've had enough blood out of me this past couple of weeks to satisfy a whole horde of vampires!'

'It's all for your own good,' she teased him, the light touch of humour winning a reluctant smile. But she could see why he had been so upset—Diane had made four or five attempts to insert the hypodermic, which must have caused him quite a lot of discomfort. It was going to be difficult to do—the veins were like threads beneath the papery skin. 'I think we'd better try the warm-water trick,' she suggested, going to fetch a bowl from the sink. 'Here, just let your arm rest in this for a few moments—it should bring up a vein. You want to get it finished before your visitors come, don't you?'

'Huh! Toadies, the whole bunch of 'em,' he scoffed dismissively. 'The only reason they come and see me is because they're after my money.'

'Oh, I'm sure that's not true,' she soothed, deftly splitting open a sterile pack and fitting the hypodermic into the syringe.

'Why else would they bother to visit an old man?' he demanded. 'To look at my handsome face?'

'Maybe it's because of your charming personality,' she suggested sweetly.

He hooted with laughter at that. 'Ah, you're a good one. Better than my whole bunch of snivelling relatives put together. Except for my son, of course,' he added with a swell of paternal pride. 'He's not at all like the rest of them. He toadies to no one!'

Megan was aware that a faint blush of pink had coloured her cheeks at the mention of the younger

Nikolaides male, but she bent over Dakis's arm, tightening the tourniquet and tapping the veins gently until she found one that seemed a little stronger than the others.

'You've met my son?' he demanded, those shrewd brown eyes focused on her face.

'Briefly.' She certainly wasn't going to tell him that he had given her a lift home last night.

'Never taken a penny off me! He started up that magazine of his all on his own—borrowed the money from a chap who owned a Chinese restaurant, of all things, and paid it all back within two years, with interest!'

'Yes, you did tell me,' she responded mildly. 'Just clench your fist for me a minute.'

'I told him when he first started it was a crazy idea. Who ever heard of anyone making money from giving something away for free? But he wouldn't listen to me. Stubborn as a mule!'

'He takes after you, then, doesn't he?' Megan teased with a gentle smile.

'Of course he does!' the old man agreed, taking her words as a compliment. 'Goes his own way, only listens to his own advice. But he gets it right! That's the important thing. He gets it right.'

She was trying not to listen too much to this paean of praise for Theo Nikolaides—even thinking about him seemed to have an odd effect on her own pulse. 'I think this one will do...' she murmured, reaching for a Sterette to swab the skin, and then slipping the needle in so gently he didn't even seem to notice. 'There! That wasn't so bad, was it?'

'Not when you do it,' he conceded grudgingly. 'Why can't the others do it as easily as that?'

'They could if you'd behave yourself.'

'Bah! You sound like a schoolmistress. I like you, though.' His eyes were narrowed, glinting with humour. 'You're sensible—you don't rush off in hysterics when a person speaks to you a little sharply. And you're a good nurse.'

'Thank you.' She smiled, pleased at the one compliment anyone could pay her that meant anything to her. Putting the sterile tray to one side, she helped Dakis sit upright while she arranged his pillows a little more comfortably. 'There—just hold your arm straight for a minute,' she reminded him, snipping off a short piece of Micropore to hold the cotton wool in place over the inside of his elbow. 'Would you like me to put the television on?'

'No, don't bother,' he grouched. 'There's nothing on worth watching—it just makes my head ache.'

'A newspaper? A book?'

'No, thank you. It's a waste of time trying to read anyway—the words just get all jumbled up on the page.'

Megan smiled. 'Well, never mind,' she consoled him. 'You'll be out of here soon, off home to Cyprus. You must be looking forward to that.'

'Huh! What is there for me to look forward to?' he demanded, refusing to see any ray of sunshine. 'I'm nothing but an old crock now. I might as well please my damned family and die.'

'You won't—only the good die young,' she retorted, knowing how to provoke him out of his glum mood. 'Besides, it wouldn't be any fun giving them what they want so easily, would it?'

That thought brought a wicked gleam to his eyes. 'No, it wouldn't,' he agreed gleefully. He lapsed into silence for a while, watching as she arranged the folds of the curtains to hang neatly in their swags. 'Listen—I've got a proposition for you,' he announced abruptly.

'Yes?'

'My family are insisting I have someone to look after me when I get out of here, but I don't want some stranger messing around with me. I want you.'

She slanted him a look of surprise. 'You mean to go back to Cyprus with you? Oh, no, I don't think so.' She shook her head. 'Thank you for the offer, but it's really not the kind of job I'm looking for. You'll have no trouble finding someone from an agency.'

'I want you,' he insisted with the petulance of one who wasn't accustomed to being denied anything. 'It's not as if it'd be hard work; it'd be more like a paid holiday—three or four months in the sun with only one patient to look after. And I'd pay you well.'

'It isn't just a question of money…'

'Damned well.' He named a figure that almost took Megan's breath away. She was about to refuse out of hand, almost annoyed that he should think she could be bought like that. But then she hesitated. She couldn't deny that it *was* tempting—she would be able to pay off her overdraft, and still have some money left over. By the time she got back, she would be able to afford to get a place of her own, instead of having to go on sharing with Cathy. And besides, she liked the old man—she could sense the loneliness behind his pride.

'I'll…think about it,' she conceded.

'How long?'

'There isn't any rush—you won't be ready for discharge just yet.'

He shook his head impatiently. 'I can't stand last-minute arrangements. Besides,' he added, a sly glint in his eyes, 'it isn't good for me to worry.'

She laughed, shaking her head. 'You old dog! That's a sneaky one to pull.'

'That's right,' he agreed with a twinkle. 'I'm used to getting my own way, and I'm too old to change now.'

'I'll think about it,' was all she would allow.

CHAPTER TWO

MEGAN was at the nurses' station, updating the patients' care plans, when the first of Dakis's nephews arrived with his family. 'Uh-oh—first act of the circus,' Sally chuckled quietly as she watched them troop past, far too full of themselves to even notice the two nurses behind the long desk. 'I just hope they don't send his blood pressure up again. Dr O'Hagan's coming round in an hour.'

Megan glanced across to the corner room. Between the half-closed slats of the blind on the door she could see the group gathered around Dakis's bed, faces solemn enough for a wake as one by one they bent to kiss him and ask solicitously after his health. No doubt the others would be here soon—they wouldn't dare risk letting Giorgos and his sour-faced wife have the field to themselves for too long.

She could understand why the old man felt their concern lacked sincerity, she mused wryly, the way they all seemed to compete with each other to see who could appear the most devoted. Melina, his youngest niece, was perhaps the nicest of the bunch, but that playboy husband of hers must be expensive to maintain. Giorgos, plump and pompous, with his piggy little eyes ever ready to perceive a slight to his dignity, Megan liked the least.

She was busy with Mrs Van Doesburgh when the others arrived, but as she passed Dakis's door a few minutes later she could see them all in there. Something seemed

25

to have upset them, too—Giorgos's wife was looking as if she had swallowed a prune, while her husband was striding around the room, pontificating about something with an air of outraged indignation.

'They're here in force today,' Sally remarked as she walked past to the linen cupboard.

'Do you think it's a good idea to let so many of them stay?' Megan asked, frowning.

'Do you fancy telling any of them they have to leave?' the ward sister countered dryly.

'Not really,' Megan confessed. And, to be honest, Dakis wasn't looking at all troubled by it. In fact he seemed to be thoroughly enjoying himself, sitting in the middle of them all, a frail figure propped up on his pillows, like some kind of venerable puppet-master pulling their strings. With a small shrug, she turned away.

A few moments later his call-bell began to beep. Sally was the nearest, so she popped in to see what he wanted, but almost at once she was out again. 'He wants you,' she told Megan.

Megan glanced up, startled. 'Why me?'

Sally shrugged. 'I've no idea. But you're his favourite—an honour to which you are more than welcome!'

Puzzled, Megan left what she was doing and went over to the corner room, tapping lightly on the door. One of the younger great-nephews was dispatched to open it for her, and stood gawping at her as she entered the room as if she had just arrived from the planet Pluto. She shot him a sharp look to remind him of his manners, and he flushed to the roots of his hair.

'Ah, there you are, *poulaki mou*,' Dakis greeted her, a note of warm affection in his voice that took her by surprise. 'Come to take good care of me, as always.'

'What do you want?' she asked, deliberately cool,

wary of the strange undercurrents she sensed in the room.

'Some more orange juice,' he responded with a beaming smile. 'If you would be so kind.'

She frowned at him, letting him see her annoyance. 'You could have asked the ward assistant for that—it's her job,' she reminded him—though she was quite sure he hadn't forgotten.

'But I want *you* to do it,' he countered, those dark eyes glinting wickedly. 'You pour such a good jug of orange juice.'

She chose not to argue with him, simply giving him a withering look as she picked up his empty jug and left the room.

Sally found her in the kitchenette at the end of the ward. 'What's going on?' she queried, frowning as she saw her opening a carton of orange juice.

'He wants a drink,' Megan responded tautly.

'Well, why are you doing it?' Sally protested. 'Carol can do it.'

'Oh, no, she can't. His lordship wants me to do it.'

The ward sister bristled visibly. 'He what? I'm not having him ordering my nurses around like that! He knows perfectly well that when there's a care assistant on duty she sorts out the drinks. My nurses have more important things to do.'

'Well, if you want to argue with him, you're welcome,' Megan remarked with a touch of humour. 'I don't suppose it'll do his blood pressure a lot of good.'

'It won't do mine a lot of good either,' Sally confessed. 'That man...!'

'Oh, he's not so bad,' Megan responded mildly. 'Anyway, it'll only take a minute.'

'Humph!' But Sally left her to it, returning to her office and the following week's shift rota, which always caused her a severe headache.

Megan emptied the carton into the jug, found a clean tumbler in the cupboard, and set them both on a small tray lined with a paper napkin. At least he wouldn't be able to complain he wasn't getting five-star service, she mused acidly. Imagine having the time to do this on a public ward!

The same young man came to open the door for her again, and she carried the tray carefully over to the bed-side table. At once one of the nieces sprang to her feet.

'Oh, Uncle Dakis—let me pour it for you,' she offered eagerly.

She received a quelling look from Giorgos's wife. 'Thank you, Melina, but *I* will pour.'

'Neither of you will pour,' Dakis announced. 'Megan will do it.' He smiled up at her, innocent as a babe— except for that wicked glint in his dark eyes. Megan returned a look of sharp suspicion; he was playing some kind of game, though she hadn't yet worked out exactly what it was.

The older woman's reaction was one of outraged indignation. 'Well! If it's not good enough to have your family pour your orange juice for you…!'

Dakis chuckled with laughter. 'Careful, Sophia— you'll pop your corsets,' he taunted her naughtily.

She sat back, closing her mouth with a snap, glaring at Megan with eyes like chips of ice. The rest of the family were stunned into silence, all of them staring at Megan as if she were the one who had uttered the insult. The only thing she could do was draw in a long, steadying breath and put on a show of icy dignity as she poured Dakis's juice and handed him the tumbler, her taut smile promising him that the matter was to be discussed later.

'There,' she purred, saccharine-sweet. 'Just call me if you need anything else.'

With a haughty tilt to her head she stalked from the room, aware of the sudden outbreak of agitated conversation—most of it in Greek—as she closed the door. Avoiding the nurses' station, where Sally would insist on knowing what had happened, she retreated to the Clean Room to check the inventory against the stores. An hour counting hypodermics and ampoules of sterile water ought to calm her down a little.

But she had barely begun her task when a peremptory male voice accosted her. She turned slowly, to confront Dakis's nephew, Giorgos, bristling with righteous self-importance.

'Can I help you?' she enquired, her fine grey eyes conveying the kind of unmistakable warning that in her last post had taught more than one bumptious young surgeon that theatre sisters were to be treated with respect.

For a moment he seemed slightly taken aback, his slack mouth gaping open. 'I...' He cleared his throat, regaining his precious dignity. 'I have something of the most importance to say to you, Miss Taylor.'

'*Nurse* Taylor,' she corrected him dryly.

'Ah! It would be well that you listen most carefully—I do not make the amusement. I am most concerned for the benefit of my respected uncle. Please do not make the mistake to think that we will stand by and allow you to make the goat of him, because he is old and has the very much money. He tells us of this plan to take you back to Cyprus with him. This we will not permit, under any circumstances. We have already the nurse hired for him, who will tend to him on his return. It is not necessary and we do not wish that you come.'

'Oh?' She was finding it difficult to maintain the façade of icy politeness over the anger that was seething inside her. 'Don't you think it's up to him who he hires?'

'It is a matter for the family,' he spluttered. 'Your conduct in this matter will most concern us, and if it is necessary it will be reported to the appropriate authorities. Do I make myself clear?'

'Perfectly.' Mrs Van Doesburgh's call-bell had begun to ring. 'Now, if you'll excuse me, one of my patients probably needs to use a bedpan.'

'Ah—good afternoon.' Dakis was sitting up in bed, his eyes wickedly bright in the thin, pale face that rested against the pillow. 'I wondered when you were going to come in and see me.'

'Oh, did you?' Megan glared at him, marching briskly across the room and setting the Dynamap apparatus down on the bedside table with somewhat unnecessary force. 'You have the nerve of the devil! What exactly have you been telling your family?'

He chuckled in rich amusement. 'I didn't tell them anything. I just sort of…encouraged them to jump to their own conclusions.'

'They're not the only ones who've been jumping to conclusions,' she countered sharply. 'I never said I was going to accept the job—and I'm certainly not going to now!'

'Why?' he taunted, his smile sly. 'Just because my stupid nephew warned you off?'

'And your son.'

'Did he really?' His eyes lit up with a gleam of satisfaction. 'Well, well—he moved quickly. Good boy!'

'"Good boy" nothing!' She hadn't intended to mention that she'd even spoken to Theo. 'They all seem to think I'm some kind of gold-digger!'

'And hasn't it got them riled up?' he gloated in delight. 'I haven't had so much fun for a long time.'

'At my expense!' she reminded him crossly, not at all gentle as she straightened his arm and wrapped the cuff of the Dynamap around it.

'Not in the least,' he argued, shaking his head. 'You're just my partner in crime.'

'Well, I'm not going to be,' she insisted darkly. 'Your nephew practically accused me of unprofessional conduct—I could get struck off the nursing register.'

'Oh, don't be silly,' he countered, dismissing her concerns with an airy wave of his hand. 'It wouldn't come to that.'

'I'm not being silly,' she asserted, reading his blood-pressure result off the Dynamap screen and marking it on his chart. 'I'm perfectly serious. I'm not going to take your job. It was very nice of you to offer...'

'I'll double the salary,' he offered, his eyes glinting like slits of polished obsidian. '*And* pay you a bonus.'

'Do you really think that will persuade me?' she demanded with icy dignity.

He smiled, undeterred by her response. 'Everyone has their price.'

'Well, I don't,' she retorted sharply. 'I'm afraid you'll have to find someone else.'

'I don't want anyone else. I want you. You're the only one that looks after me the way I like...'

'It's a bit too late to try that line now,' she retorted without sympathy, and, gathering up the Dynamap, she marched from the room.

The car park was just visible from the small window at the far end of the ward corridor, so Megan was able to keep half an eye open for the sleek dark blue Aston Martin as she went about her afternoon chores. As soon as she spotted it, she found an excellent excuse to make herself scarce by going to get Mrs Van Doesburgh's room ready for her return from X-Ray.

But as she heard the sound of those familiar footsteps striding through the ward she couldn't help but glance up from her task. Those vividly blue eyes caught hers for a brief moment as he passed the door, with a look which should have withered the expensive bouquet of yellow roses in their vase on the dressing table. She returned him a cold stare, hoping he wouldn't notice the faint, betraying blush of pink in her cheeks, and turned all her attention to the task in hand.

It was only because he had been so rude to her that his presence caused her pulse to race in that alarming way, she excused herself rationally—that and the memory of the way he had looked at her when he had caught her in the sluice, in that unintentionally provocative pose that had shown off rather too much of her long, slender legs.

Of course he was attractive, she acknowledged with a cool detachment—she couldn't deny that. But it didn't affect her personally any more than it did to watch some chisel-featured movie star on the cinema screen. And, from the two fleeting encounters she had had with him, she had enough evidence to decide that as a person she didn't like him.

Yesterday's rain had given way to a pleasant spring afternoon, so when she had finished making up the bed she went over to open the window and air the room. It was then that she realised that the window was at right angles to Dakis's window, in the corner of the building, and that his window was also open. The voices she could hear made it clear that he and his son were quarrelling again.

'You don't need me to take it on,' she heard Theo say. 'You've got several perfectly good managers in the hotels—why not promote one of them?'

Dakis responded with a flood of Greek. Though she couldn't understand the words, the tone was unmistakably one of impatience.

'All right,' Theo countered, again in English, 'if you insist on it being one of the family, what about one of my sainted cousins? Most of them would sell their own children for the chance.'

'That useless bunch of misbegotten she-donkeys?' Dakis snorted in disgust. 'How did my own sisters come to spawn such spineless jellyfish? They'd run everything bankrupt inside of six months.'

'Well, I'm not interested,' Theo insisted with what sounded like a yawn. 'I have my own business interests here in England, in case you'd forgotten.'

'Hah! You have your…English *tsoules*, that is what it is! It is time you accepted your responsibilities to your family—found yourself a decently behaved girl, raised some fine grandsons for me. A man should at least have the chance to bounce his first grandson on his knee before he dies.'

Theo laughed. It was a very attractive laugh, low and husky, and implicitly sensual—and Megan felt an odd little frisson of heat shiver down her spine. She really shouldn't be eavesdropping like this—it was hardly professional conduct. Besides, she had a great deal of work to do…

'Oh, I'll marry in my own good time,' Theo remarked with the casual arrogance of one who knew how wide a field was his for the choosing. 'Anyway, if we are talking of *tsoules*, you should be the expert. What about that peroxided little popsy you're planning to take home with you?'

Megan bridled. She didn't know what '*tsoules*' meant, but she was ready to bet that it wasn't particularly flattering. And she needed no interpreter for 'popsy'. She felt her palm itch with a sudden, uncharacteristic urge to slap that handsome face.

'She's not a popsy.' Dakis sprang instantly to her defence. 'She's a proper nurse. I need a nurse to look after me. I won't be well for quite a while yet—if ever.'

Theo remained unmoved by the note of pathos in his father's wavering voice. 'You old fool,' he scoffed mockingly. 'She's probably only after your money.'

'So what?' Dakis retorted, petulant. 'It's my money—it's up to me how I spend it. Besides, I shall like to have a pretty girl around. She is pretty, isn't she?' he added slyly.

'It'd serve you right if she took you for every penny you've got,' Theo retorted with a snap of impatience. 'And if you can't see it coming you must be going senile!'

A hot fury sizzled through Megan's veins, firing her into action before she had even stopped to consider. Darting over to the mirror above the dressing table, she snatched off her cap, dragging the pins from her hair and tousling it with her fingers into a just-got-out-of-bed wildness. A slick of Mrs Van Doesburgh's scarlet lipstick and a generous splash of her exotic perfume added to the image, and for good measure she tightened the belt of her uniform an extra notch, and unfastened the top button to draw attention to her slender curves.

'*Peroxide popsy*, eh?' she snarled at her own reflection. 'You arrogant pig! It's time someone taught you a thing or two, Theo Nikolaides!'

A small voice inside her head warned her that this was probably a very stupid idea, but she was too angry to be rational. Glancing swiftly out into the corridor to check that no one was in sight, she slipped around the corner to Dakis's room. Someone had to intervene in the quarrel before it did the old man some harm, she excused herself. At least this would make him laugh.

'Now, now, what's all this fuss?' she purred, entering without knocking. 'You know you're not supposed to get yourself all worked up, Daki, darling.'

For an instant she was afraid that the startled look in his eyes would give the game away, but as she leaned over to rearrange his pillows he gave her a mischievous wink. 'It's just my way of getting you to come in and see me, *poulaki mou*,' he chuckled.

A sound from behind her could have been a snort of disgust. She giggled, wriggling in the over-tightened uniform—she ought to get an Oscar for this, at the very least. 'Ah, now, Daki, that's naughty. You know I have other patients to look after,' she protested, pouting.

'But I'm your favourite, aren't I?' the old man declared, patting her neatly rounded *derrière*—a liberty that under normal circumstances she would have permitted no one even to dream of taking. Her eyes flashed him a swift warning not to go too far, but she kept up the act, drawing on her sister Cathy, at her most outrageously flirtatious, for inspiration.

'Of course you are,' she cooed. 'But what were you arguing about?'

'My son thinks I'm senile,' he informed her gleefully.

'He what?' She shot the younger man a look of reproach, somewhat undermined by the flutter of her eye-lashes. 'Of course you're not. What a silly thing to say!'

Those deep blue eyes were darkened by storm-clouds, the hard jaw set like steel. 'If he thinks hiring you as a nurse is going to do his health any good, "senile" is the politest word for him I can think of,' he grated harshly.

'She's done me a great deal of good already,' Dakis declared. 'She's the best nurse I've ever had.'

'She certainly has her own unique bedside manner,' Theo returned, letting his cool gaze slide down over her in an assessment that was a calculated insult. 'Though whether it's in any of the nursing manuals I take leave to doubt.'

'I'll be a lot better off with her than with the kind of po-faced old harridan you'd be likely to hire.'

'At least a po-faced old harridan wouldn't be more interested in your bank account than your blood pressure.'

'Don't you believe it. They're usually the worst sort.'

'Not if I'm responsible for hiring them, they're not.'

'Anyway, Daki knows I'm not after his money, don't you, Daki?' Megan intervened, her voice so honeyed it would have had difficulty passing the food and drugs administration. 'I'd never even dream of such a thing!'

'And you can have a good game of snowballs in hell!' Theo snapped back at her. 'And that's where I'll see you before you get one penny of my father's money!'

'It's my money!' Dakis protested, indignant. 'It's my business what I do with it. You're not interested enough to want to come into the company, so you can just leave me to get on with it in whatever way I choose.'

'Fine,' Theo ground out, close to exploding. 'If that's the way you want it, that's fine by me.' He stalked from the room, closing the door with a controlled slam.

Megan shook her head. 'Well, I hope you're pleased with that,' she remarked, pulling her cap from her pocket and attempting to fix it back on her head. 'You've really annoyed him now.'

'Obstinate young fool,' Dakis grumbled irritably.

'Hark who's talking!'

The old man chuckled, acknowledging her point. 'Ah, but he'll come into line now, just you see. He's taken it for granted up till now that he can act the playboy, but seeing his inheritance in danger of being whipped away from right under his nose will make him take his responsibilities a little more seriously!'

'Is that what all this is really about?' she queried, frowning. 'To persuade your son to go back to Cyprus and join you in the family business?'

'Of course! You should have seen his face! I think he wanted to strangle you!'

'I *did* see his face,' Megan murmured dryly—and he had looked as if he would have favoured a much slower form of torture. A slow spit-roast over an open fire, kebab-style, perhaps? She shook her head firmly. 'I'm sorry, Dakis, but it really isn't me. I'm afraid you'll have to get someone else to play the role.'

That wicked glint sparked in his eyes again. 'Ah, but you can't back out now,' he insisted gleefully. 'He'll think he's scared you off!'

'Why, you sly old goat!' she protested, forced to concede the truth of his words—and startled by her own stupid reluctance to let Theo Nikolaides believe anything of the sort.

Dakis chuckled again, recognising his triumph. 'I told you, I'm too old not to get my own way.'

But Megan doubted that he would get his own way

with his son. He didn't strike her as the type to come to heel so easily.

By the time Megan finished her shift she was exhausted, and looking forward to nothing more than a long, hot bath, and two days off before she started a week on the night-shift. The brief spell of sunshine had already given way to cold April showers again—it certainly made the thought of spending three or four months in Cyprus *very* tempting…

But as she turned the corner from the bus stop she stopped dead in her tracks, groaning in horror. A dark blue Aston Martin was parked at the kerb right outside the front entrance of the block of flats where she lived—and she had little hope that it would turn out to belong to someone else. For a moment she was strongly tempted to turn around and walk the other way, but she knew she was going to have to confront him sooner or later, so it might as well be now. Squaring her shoulders, she marched across the road.

The block, like its neighbours, had been quite run-down until a few years ago, but, since the area had become popular with media types and the bright young things who worked in the nearby City offices, it had been bought up by a property company and restored to something like its former glory.

There was no sign of Theo in the imposing entrance hall, with its art-deco grandeur and imitation-marble floor—which meant that he had probably persuaded Cathy to let him into the flat. Damn, he had a nerve! And what was Cathy thinking of? She had never even set eyes on him before—for all she knew, he could be an axe-murderer or something!

Her fears were confirmed as soon as she entered the

flat. The door to the sitting room flew open, and Cathy bounced out into the hall, startling in a green satin micro-skirt and purple tights, her improbable magenta-streaked hair backcombed into a wild fuzz, her kohl-rimmed eyes sparkling with merriment. 'Ah—there you are at last! Well, aren't you the dark horse?'

'I beg your pardon?' Megan queried, startled.

Cathy nodded towards the sitting room behind her. 'He's in there,' she whispered conspiratorially. 'Don't worry, I managed to keep my hands off him—just. He's absolutely gorgeous! Anyway, you can have the place all to yourself—I'm going straight on to the gig with Luther, and there's a party after, so I doubt if I'll be back. Don't do anything I wouldn't do!' She giggled as she sailed out of the door. 'That gives you plenty of scope!'

Warily Megan pushed open the door to the sitting room. Theo Nikolaides was lounging on the leather chesterfield, a cup of coffee at his elbow, looking as if he had taken literally an invitation to make himself at home. She glared at him in icy anger. 'What are you doing here?' she demanded. 'How did you know where I live?'

He shrugged his wide shoulders in a gesture of casual disdain. 'It was easy enough to find out,' he responded lazily. 'In fact it was easy to find out anything I wanted to know about you. And any information I lacked, your delightfully forthright sister was more than willing to supply.'

'You've been spying on me!' she accused acidly.

That hard mouth curved into a smile of lazy mockery. 'If you can't stand the heat, you should learn not to play with fire. I did warn you that I could be dangerous. Did you think I was joking?' He rose easily to his feet, seeming to dominate the room with his presence as he wandered around, examining the books on the bookshelf, the crystals Cathy kept on the ornate marble mantelpiece. He picked up a photograph in a silver frame. 'Your parents?'

'Put that down!'

'You don't have any photographs of Jeremy, I see. Or have you thrown them all away?'

She felt her cheeks colour a heated red. 'Who told you about Jeremy?'

'Who do you think? A mine of information, your sister. Why did you ditch him, I wonder? According to Cathy he was *very* handsome. A doctor, too—very eligible. *And* comfortably off. But perhaps "comfortably off" wasn't quite enough for you.' He let his glance rove lazily around the spacious room, which was somewhat bizarrely furnished according to Cathy's eclectic taste. 'It must be quite a struggle, paying the rent on a place like this on a nurse's salary. But then who can blame you for wanting the best out of life? Or for wanting a better pay-off for all that training and dedication?'

She met that mocking gaze defiantly. It was pointless to try to defend herself—he had already tried her and found her guilty, even before that rather foolish little charade she had played out at Dakis's bedside. 'That's my business,' she retorted with cool dignity.

'Oh, no.' He shook his head, taking a menacing pace towards her. 'You made it my business when you set your sights on my father and his money. He doesn't need your kind of nursing.'

She found herself forced into retreating a step as he came closer, but she refused to let him intimidate her. 'That's...for him to decide,' she countered, struggling to keep her voice steady.

'No, Miss Taylor—it's for you to decide. I think when

you give the matter your most careful consideration you will conclude that it is in your own best interests to turn down my father's foolish offer. I don't take kindly to being crossed.'

'And I don't take kindly to being threatened, Mr Nikolaides.'

'You don't? Then perhaps you need a little demonstration, just to warn you that I mean what I say. And that I fight dirty.'

Before she had time to realise what he was going to do, he had reached out a hand and caught her by the hair, dragging her head ruthlessly back. For one moment those vivid blue eyes blazed fiercely down into hers, and then his mouth was crushing hers, and she tasted the salty tang of her own blood as she was forced to yield, parting her lips beneath the onslaught of his kiss.

She tried to twist away from him, but she was trapped, her body curved hard against his as his other hand slid down to rest with an insolent assumption of intimacy on the base of her spine, making her devastatingly aware that her struggles were serving only to arouse him. And he wasn't the only one, she realised with a small shock—as she felt those strong arms around her, subduing with ease her every attempt to break free, she was conscious of something primitive inside her that was beginning to respond.

He sensed her surrender before she was aware of it herself, and his kiss gentled, becoming more tender and infinitely more dangerous, a deeply sensual invasion of her mouth, exploring every sensitive corner with his languorous tongue. With every breath the evocative, musky scent of his skin was drugging her mind, undermining any thoughts she might have had of trying to resist.

His hand had risen to cup her breast, moulding and

caressing its ripe, round shape, and she moaned softly, unable to find the will to stop him as he crushed it deliciously beneath his palm, the tender nipple hardening to a taut bud that sizzled with an incandescent heat.

Some sane part of her mind was trying to tell her that she shouldn't be allowing this to happen, but her treacherous body wanted only to continue, to have him sweep her up in his strong arms and carry her through to the bedroom, to strip her naked and crush her beneath his weight, to make real the fevered dreams that had disturbed her sleep so badly last night...

But abruptly he pulled back, his breathing ragged and harsh. 'So—now you know that I know exactly what kind of woman you are,' he ground out, that cold blue gaze a whiplash of contempt as it slid down over her—and with a rush of shame she became aware that he had unfastened several of the buttons down the front of her uniform. She hadn't even realised he'd been doing it. 'Be warned—leave my father alone, or I shall ensure that you rue the day you chose to cross me.'

And with those words he stalked from the room, slamming the door behind him, leaving her shaking with reaction. Weakly she sat down on the sofa, pulling her clothing straight as she struggled to steady the racing beat of her heart.

CHAPTER THREE

THE ENGLISH CHANNEL slid away slowly beneath the white wing of the luxurious private Lear jet. Megan sipped the glass of mineral water the stewardess had brought her, gazing out of the window as they slowly overtook a hovercraft racing beneath them, its wake a white streak across the blue-grey water.

She had never travelled in this sort of style before. From the chauffeur-driven Rolls-Royce that had come to pick her up—much to Cathy's envy—it had been cosseted comfort all the way. She had expected that they would fly from Heathrow, or perhaps Gatwick, so it had been a surprise when, instead of heading out along the M4 motorway, they had turned up through Perivale, until they had reached a leafy suburb, and a private airstrip.

Though she should have guessed, she reflected, glancing across at Dakis, who was already beginning to doze, tired by even the short journey from the hospital. Even when he was well, she couldn't imagine him having the patience to bother with tedious things like flight schedules and boarding gates, even if he was travelling first-class. He had the money, so he made his own rules.

There were seats for ten on the plane, but they were the only two passengers. Dakis had refused point-blank to allow Giorgos or any of his other nephews and nieces to fly back to Cyprus with them. 'I never asked you to come over in the first place,' he had told them rudely to their faces. 'You got here under your own steam—you can go back under your own steam.'

She hadn't seen Theo for more than a week—not since that night he had come to her flat, in fact. He had gone to New York, Dakis had told her—a respite for which she was more than grateful. Even the memory of the way he had kissed her, and the way she had responded so wantonly, could still bring a blush of shame to her cheeks.

It had cost her a lot of sleepless nights, wondering if she should just tell Dakis that she had changed her mind, and couldn't accept the job after all. But some kind of obstinate streak had refused to allow her to back down in such a cowardly way in the face of his son's threats—that, and a frosty letter from the bank reminding her that she had reached the limit of her overdraft, which could not be further extended.

So, she had made her decision—it was just that a small, niggling voice inside her head kept whispering that she had made a very big mistake. With Theo in New York, she had been able to persuade herself that she really wasn't afraid of him, that he had only been able to do what he had done that night because she had been tired, and hadn't been expecting him to kiss her. Next time she would be ready to defend herself, with whatever it took… But she didn't feel as confident of that as she would have liked.

The plane banked slightly as they crossed the coast of Belgium, and then settled once again onto a steady flight-path, high above the rich green fields of the Low Countries. But as they approached the Ardennes a blanket of low cloud rolled in, hiding the land beneath. She turned back from the window with a yawn; the soft, steady note of the engines, and the warmth in the cabin—not to mention too many restless nights—were making her sleepy.

Her eyes were almost closed, but she was conscious that someone had come through from the flight-deck—the pilot, probably, coming to have a word with the cabin-crew. She took little notice—until he sat down beside her, and her nostrils instantly recognised the musky male scent of his skin.

She sat up sharply, her eyes wide with shock. 'What…are you doing here?' she demanded raggedly.

'I'm flying the plane.'

'You're *what*…?'

Those deep blue eyes glinted with sardonic humour. 'Well, co-pilot, at least,' he responded laconically. 'I need to keep up my flying hours to retain my European licence.'

'I…thought you were still in New York,' she protested weakly. 'Dakis never mentioned…that you were back.'

'Perhaps he suspected that you might change your mind if you knew I'd be coming along,' he suggested, his voice laced with mockery.

She was beginning to recover her composure a little, and returned him a look of cool indifference. 'Why should I do that?'

'Perhaps your sense of self-preservation might have got the better of your greed.'

She shrugged her slender shoulders, defiantly casual in the face of his implicit warning. Dakis seemed to be asleep, his breathing deep and even; the cabin-crew were in the galley at the back of the plane. They were alone, but not alone; even so, it was probably foolish to provoke him, the rational part of her mind urged cautiously. But it was difficult to be rational when he was around. Besides, attack was the best form of defence—at the moment, it was the only form of defence she could think of.

He was watching her, those shrewd blue eyes seemingly able to read every thought that passed through her head. 'Why did you choose to defy me?' he asked softly.

'I didn't,' she countered, icily cool. 'I chose to ignore you.'

He quirked one dark eyebrow, amused by the challenge in her response. 'Did you think I didn't mean what I said?' he questioned, his voice quiet, but with an unmistakable hint of menace. 'Or maybe you were hoping I'd offer you money to stay away from my father. I'm afraid you'll be disappointed. I have no intention of bribing a woman like you.'

'Why would I accept a bribe?' she retorted, stung into reckless anger by his insulting words. 'It would only be a fraction of what I could get out of your father.'

'True,' he conceded tautly. 'But, on the other hand, you could find yourself with nothing at all.'

'Maybe I like gambling.'

'You'll need to. You're playing for very high stakes.'

'Of course. It's no fun playing for peanuts.'

'How very true. And you'll be playing on my ground.' He rose easily to his feet. 'Don't be deceived by all the tourist brochures of Cyprus. It may put on a sunny face, but scratch the surface and it's still almost a medieval society, with medieval values. *Yá sas.*'

He disappeared through the door that led to the flight-deck, leaving Megan shaking as she struggled to still the painful racing of her heart. She must have been crazy to get herself involved in this stupid charade—if she had a crumb of sense she'd get herself on a flight back to England the minute the plane landed.

'That was good.' Startled, she glanced across at Dakis.

His eyelids were still half-closed, but beneath them his eyes glinted with amused satisfaction. 'You almost had me believing you!'

She shot him a look of angry reproach. 'I thought you were asleep.'

'Only a little bit. You were enjoying making my son angry, I think.'

She was conscious that her cheeks were tinged faintly with pink, but she shook her head. 'He's even ruder than you are! I just hope when this silly game of yours is all over you'll tell him the truth.'

He chuckled richly. 'Ah, it will all be taken care of. Now, I think we will have a little something to eat, yes? And then I really will sleep, if you will excuse me. We will be another four hours or so flying, but we should be at my home in time for dinner.'

'Well, you might have been a fool for coming here, but you can't complain about this!'

It was only a little after seven in the morning, but already it was quite warm enough for Megan to stand on the wide stone balcony outside her bedroom wearing only her cotton pyjamas. The sky was a clear, vivid blue, with not even a wisp of a cloud. And the sea was even bluer—the clear, deep blue of sapphires, barely rippled by a wave, sparkling in the early-morning sunshine.

She drew in a long, deep breath, catching a hint of the piquant scent of juniper on the air. The villa stood on a low rise of ground, a few kilometres along the coast from the town of Limassol, but so secluded that it could have been on its own private island. Below her the garden was a patchwork of terraces and bright flowerbeds, sloping gently down towards a small beach of pebbles and sharp, dark sand, lapped by the whispering waves of the southern Mediterranean.

On a sudden impulse she turned back into her room, and ran across to slide open the louvred door that led into a beautifully appointed dressing room and *en-suite* bathroom. The maid who had unpacked her cases last night had stowed all her clothes neatly in the vast fitted wardrobes, all beautifully built from light beech wood. A dressing room of her own, and a maid to unpack her cases! She really had fallen into the lap of luxury here, she reflected with a touch of wry humour.

Her swimsuit, chain-store bought and inexpensive, brought her down to earth. She was only here for a little while—twelve or fourteen weeks at most—and she was as much an employee as the maid. But while she was here she might as well make the most of it. Tossing her pyjamas onto the bed, she pulled on the swimsuit and slipped a loose cotton shirt around her shoulders, and then, snatching up a huge, fluffy towel from the stack in the bathroom, she set off to find her way down to the gardens.

The villa was built in two wings, which angled back slightly towards the sea from a vast central atrium tiled in shimmering pale gold marble. The southern wall and the high roof were both made entirely of glass that had a bronze tint to let the sunlight flood in, but not its glare or heat. At the first-floor level a plant-lined veranda ran round from the corridors that led to the bedrooms, to meet at the head of a wide black marble staircase that led down to the ground floor.

There was a lift, but Megan chose to skip down the stairs. To her left were the main family rooms—the dining room where they had eaten last night, a spacious sitting room with a glass wall that folded back to give access straight onto the gardens, a room that housed Dakis's impressive collection of antiquities gathered from all over the island, and several other smaller rooms that Megan hadn't explored yet.

The other wing of the ground floor she understood to contain mostly offices, but Dakis had told her there was also an indoor swimming pool and a gymnasium that she could use whenever she wanted. But this morning she preferred to try the sea, so, crossing to the wide doors that led out to the garden, she walked down the path, exchanging a smile and a rather clumsily pronounced '*Kaliméra*' with the gardener who was tending to a colourful patch of begonias beneath the shade of a whispering casuarina.

The sand crunched between her toes as she walked across it, dropping her shirt on top of her towel and hurrying on excitedly to the water's edge. But as the first wavelets rippled over her foot she skipped back in shock. It might look warm, but it was freezing! Perhaps this wasn't such a good idea, after all—the indoor pool might be better.

But as she half turned to walk back up the beach she realised that she had an audience—Theo. He was standing on one of the balconies on the far wing from hers—and even from this distance she could see the mocking smile curving that hard mouth.

'Good morning,' he called to her, a sardonic inflection in his voice.

'Hi!' She waved brightly. 'Lovely morning. Why don't you come in for a swim?'

'I'm afraid the sea's still a little cold for me to take an early-morning dip at this time of the year—I prefer the pool.' A sweep of his hand drew her attention to what she had missed—a large, irregularly shaped swimming pool tucked into the landscaping of the garden. 'But you're obviously braver than me. Enjoy!'

She knew he was taunting her—and she knew she didn't have to take it as a challenge. But her stupid pride wouldn't let her back down. Gritting her teeth—from this distance it could look like a smile—she turned back to face the deceptively welcoming water. 'Dammit, dammit, dammit…' Closing her eyes, she forced herself forward into a run, splashing into the icy waves.

Her voice rose in a shriek, which she turned into a laugh, plunging forward and diving, her breath paralysed by the cold, her skin stinging. It was even colder beneath the surface, where the sun's rays hadn't reached, and she came up quickly, striking out with a powerful stroke, hoping that if she kept moving she might warm up a little.

It was like some form of torture—self-inflicted—but she forced herself to endure it. She was not going to let him think she was chicken—however stupid she knew she was being. Rolling onto her back, she could see that Theo had left the balcony and come down to the beach, and she waved again, her teeth chattering too much to call out to him.

'Come out!' he shouted, a sharp edge in his voice. 'It's much too cold—you'll get cramp.'

'Don't be silly!' she called back, laughing. 'It's lovely.'

'You stupid… If I have to come in there and get you…!'

She knew he was right—already there were sharp pains in her arms and legs. She was reluctant to come out of the water while he was standing there watching her, but she had no choice—another few minutes and she could be in serious difficulties. Finding her feet on the sandy bottom, she stood up.

The water came to just below her waist, and she knew that the icy cold had tautened her breasts, stinging the tender nipples into taut buds that were plainly visible beneath the wet, clinging jersey of her swimsuit. She was acutely conscious of those blue eyes lingering there in insolent appreciation, the glint of mocking amusement in them telling her that he was thoroughly enjoying her discomfort.

She made herself walk forward, her body rising slowly out of the water. A coil of tension was knotting in her stomach, but she had nowhere to hide—she was forced to accept that blatantly sexual appraisal as he let his gaze drift down over every slender curve. She could only hold her head at a haughty angle, struggling to pretend that she wasn't the least bit disturbed by him.

He picked up her towel and came towards her, his expression changing to one of sharp impatience. 'Okay, what were you trying to prove?' he demanded, wrapping the towel around her and beginning to rub her vigorously dry.

'N-nothing. I was j-just having a s-swim.' Her teeth were chattering violently now, and in spite of the brisk friction of the towel she felt as if she would never get warm again.

'The sun may be shining, but we're not even halfway through April yet. You must be crazy!'

'No, I'm not.' Her eyes flashed with annoyance, and, stepping back out of his grasp, she began to scrub herself with the towel. 'I didn't realise it was going to be quite as cold as that, that's all. But it was a good swim, and now I'm ready for my breakfast.'

And, snatching up her shirt, she stalked away up the

beach, her head held high, though her numbed legs were barely able to respond to her commands.

The bath water was deliciously warm, bringing life back into Megan's frozen limbs. She had poured in a generous splash of a fragranced bath-oil that she had found on the shelf, just to add to the sensation of blissful luxury, and she closed her eyes, feeling the numb ache of cold slowly melt away.

She would have preferred not to think about the way Theo had looked at her, but it was impossible to put it out of her mind. She had felt as though she was naked, and even now her soft skin seemed to tingle at the memory of that insolent gaze sliding down over every curve of her body, caressing her...

A low moan broke from her lips, and she shook her head, struggling to dispel the disturbing image. If she was going to see out her contract, she was going to have to find a way to reinforce her defences against him. He was far too astute not to recognise the effect he had on her—and far too ruthless to have any scruples about using it to his advantage.

Clambering out of the bath, she scrubbed herself briskly dry with one of the huge fluffy towels, and chose a yellow cotton dress from the wardrobe. Her hair was still damp, so she caught it back from her face with a white bandeau and left it to dry naturally in the warmth of the day. Then she went back downstairs in search of breakfast.

She found Dakis and Theo sitting at a table on the terrace. Dakis glanced up, beaming in delight at the sight of her. 'Ha! You see? I was up before you this morning,' he announced proudly.

'On the contrary,' Theo informed him dryly. 'Nurse

Taylor has already been for a very refreshing swim—in the sea.'

'In the sea, eh? Brave girl! Bit chilly, was it?'

'A little,' she admitted, her eyes evading Theo's mocking gaze.

'Well, have some coffee,' Dakis invited, indicating the empty chair beside him. 'That'll soon warm you up.' Showing off his returning abilities, he carefully set a cup and saucer in front of her, and lifted the lid of the coffee-pot to peer inside. 'Damn—it's nearly empty.'

'I'll go and fetch some more,' she suggested at once, jumping to her feet again.

He stared at her in blank astonishment. 'Sit down! Paria will fetch it.' He raised his voice, bellowing the maid's name so loudly she could have heard it if she'd been on the far side of the island.

The young girl came scuttling out from the kitchen, her eyes wide with apprehension, and darted to the table to pick up the pot, scurrying away again to obey the order as if she feared eternal damnation at the very least.

Even after witnessing the way he had behaved in hospital, Megan had been a little shocked by Dakis's bullying manner towards his staff. Last night she had excused him with the recollection that he must be very tired after the journey, but it seemed that it was continuing unabated. Her thoughts must have shown in her eyes, because she caught Theo watching her, faintly amused.

'I think Nurse Taylor disapproves of you, Papa,' he remarked with the air of one wielding a large wooden spoon to stir up trouble.

'Disapproves? Why?'

She shot Theo a fulminating glare, and patted Dakis's hand soothingly. 'I was just concerned about you shouting like that. It isn't good for you to let yourself get agitated.'

His expression was blank and uncomprehending. 'Agitated? I was simply calling the maid to do her job. What is wrong with that? They just sit around gossiping if they have not enough work to do.'

'Perhaps you could get a bell?' she suggested sweetly. 'That would make it a lot easier.'

He snapped his fingers. 'I know! I shall have one of those two-way radios they use in the hotels. Every one of them can have a set, and then there can be no excuses that they do not hear me calling. Why did I not think of that before? It is perfect! You can sort it out, Theo.'

Theo shook his head. 'I'm afraid I have to go back to London this afternoon, Papa.'

Dakis frowned sharply. 'So soon? You're not even staying for a few days?'

'I would like to, but I'm afraid something important has cropped up.'

'Dammit, what could be more important than taking care of your own father when he's ill?' Dakis demanded, indignant.

There was the faintest hint of mockery in Theo's smile. 'You don't need me to take care of you, Papa. You have the estimable Nurse Taylor at your disposal—having insisted so forcefully on hiring her.'

The old man looked furious at being cornered. 'It is not the same thing at all, and you know it! Well, fine, if that's the attitude you want to take. Go on, you might as well leave now. Leave me by myself, if you don't care what happens to me. I'll try not to die at a time that's inconvenient to you—I wouldn't want people to think you were too busy to come to your own father's funeral...'

Megan, anxious, leaned across and took his hand again. 'Dakis, don't let yourself get worked up,' she coaxed gently. She slanted an acid glance across the table at Theo. 'Do you have to always argue with him like this?'

Theo laughed, and rose to his feet. 'I appear to be outnumbered. Perhaps I had better retreat. I'll see you before I leave, Papa.'

'Don't bother yourself!'

'You never could resist making a Greek tragedy out of everything.'

'I am Greek—Greek Cypriot! I've never denied it—which is more than I can say for you.'

'I've never denied my Greek half,' his son responded evenly. 'But I won't deny my English half, either. And the sooner you realise that, the better.' He turned and strolled away, his long, athletic stride easy and relaxed, as if the argument had never taken place.

After breakfast, Megan spent some time trying to coax Dakis to practise his exercises. But he was impatient, and tired quickly, so instead she suggested a game of table draughts. It was as much as he could do to concentrate on the simple game, but his fiercely competitive streak wouldn't let him lose, so in that way she managed to keep him occupied for most of the morning.

They had lunch on the terrace, and then she managed to persuade him to take a nap. Though he grumbled at the suggestion, accusing her of treating him like an old man, she suspected that in truth he was more than ready to lie down for a couple of hours.

It took a while to settle him comfortably, with a pillow beneath his half-paralysed left arm and another beneath his knee to keep his muscles properly flexed. She drew the curtains across the windows, left some music playing softly to soothe him to sleep, and as she tiptoed quietly from the room the sound of his breathing had already settled into a slow, regular pattern.

Carefully closing the door, she turned away—and almost collided with Theo. There had been no sign of him since breakfast, and she had more or less assumed that he had already left. 'Oh! You…startled me,' she gasped, struggling to keep her voice steady.

'I'm sorry. I was going to go and say goodbye to my father.'

'Well, you should have done it earlier,' she returned on a note of caustic censure. 'He's asleep now.'

That hard mouth curved into a smile of cynical mockery. 'Good little nursey—settled him down, have you? You seemed to be an awfully long time in there.'

She chose to ignore the cheap innuendo. 'You're leaving, then?' she enquired frostily.

'I'm afraid so. Will you miss me?'

'I won't, but he will.' She nodded in the direction of the closed door.

He laughed without humour, his eyes cold. 'He'll get over it.'

Megan sighed, shaking her head. 'Why do you have to argue with him all the time?' she asked wearily, starting to walk towards the stairs.

'He enjoys it.'

She glanced up at him, wishing that she could somehow find a way to persuade either of these two proud, obstinate men to take that one step towards the other, to overcome the lingering bitterness of the past. 'He's very serious about wanting you to take over the company, you know,' she told him quietly. 'He really believes you're the only person who can run it successfully.'

Theo shrugged his wide shoulders in a gesture of casual unconcern. 'I will one day.'

She stopped, startled, staring up at him. 'When?' she demanded.

'When I'm sure he won't interfere,' he responded bluntly.

She was forced to concede that he had a point. His father was making a good recovery from his stroke—he was still inclined to get tired very quickly, and he had some lingering problems with concentration and spatial awareness, but those symptoms would fade. Within a couple of months, if he continued to make such good progress, he would be almost back to his old self. And he certainly wasn't ready to retire.

'So—how long will you be away?' she asked as casually as she could.

'I don't know. A few weeks, maybe.'

She slanted him a dry look. 'I'm surprised you're willing to risk leaving me here, since you're so suspicious of my motives,' she remarked.

He laughed lazily, smiling down at her in genuine amusement. 'I don't have much choice. Besides, you won't have an open field. My sainted cousin Giorgos will be descending on you shortly, and I doubt the rest of the bunch will be far behind. I wish you well of them.' With one finger he tilted up her chin, and brushed a light, mocking kiss across her lips. 'Have fun.'

Theo's prediction about Giorgos proved deadly accurate. He arrived the next day with his supercilious wife, Sophia, in tow, announcing plans to stay at the villa for an extended visit—a suggestion which did little for Dakis's temper. They had brought with them Sophia's niece, a doe-eyed young girl of about nineteen or twenty called Eleni.

Dinner that evening was fraught. First Giorgos voiced his blunt opinion that Megan had no place at the family dinner table, and should take her meals in the kitchen with the other servants, which prompted Dakis to tell him rudely to mind his own business. Then Sophia remarked that she was surprised that Theo had chosen to return to London when his place was clearly at his sick father's bedside, which produced a string of invective in jumbled Greek and English to the effect that Giorgos need not look to a place in running the company because the executive offices did not have appropriate accommodation for a donkey.

It was a relief when the meal was finally over, and Megan was able to coax Dakis into having an early night. After she had helped him into bed, settling him into a reasonably comfortable position, she gave him his tablets—adding a mild sedative to help him sleep. He took it without comment—she wasn't sure that he had even noticed.

She was almost tempted to take one herself, but instead she decided to go for a stroll in the garden. It was a beautiful evening; there was just a slight breeze, barely enough to stir her hair. The warm air was sweet with the fragrance of jasmine and lavender, and as she moved further from the house the only sound was the soft whisper of the sea as it lapped against the secluded beach.

She walked right down to the water's edge, and stood gazing out towards the dark horizon. There was no moon, which made the stars seem more bright, like a million tiny diamonds spilled across a swathe of black velvet. With a small sigh she brushed the hair back from her face. It was so romantic, so sad to be standing here alone…

'Hello…?'

She turned sharply as Eleni came up behind her. For no particular reason, she had taken an instant dislike to the younger girl—perhaps because she seemed to be trying a little too hard to be sweet. But she managed some sort of smile. 'Oh… Hello.'

'You do not mind that I join you?' Eleni asked confidingly. 'I should have gone to bed, but I am not yet tired.'

Megan forced herself to suppress her irritation. After all, she could scarcely tell the girl to go away.

Eleni trod delicately down over the sand to the water's edge, careful not to get close enough to the sea to get her dainty silver sandals wet. She was actually quite a pretty girl, Megan acknowledged, but there was something affected about her mannerisms—particularly the way she kept moving her head to swing her sleek, jaw-length bob of black hair around, as if to call attention to its shining perfection.

'I'm sorry about Aunt Sophia,' she cooed, peeping up through her fringe. 'I am afraid she can be rather… I'm sorry, I do not have very good English. Stuck-up? Is that the word?'

'Probably,' Megan responded.

'I did not mind that you were there,' the girl went on earnestly. 'I like to practise my English. I am from Greece, not Cyprus, but I must learn to speak good English. I would like very much to live in London. I have been to visit, but only with my aunt and uncle, and they would not let me go out by myself. It must be so exciting to live there.'

Megan shrugged. 'It's pretty much like any other city, I suppose. Noisy, crowded, too much traffic…'

'Oh, but the shops are so wonderful! I went to Oxford Street with Aunt Sophia, and I could have spent my whole allowance in one afternoon! And then there are the nightclubs, I think. Annabel's—I tried to persuade my cousin Theo to take me, but he would not. He is as strict as my aunt Sophia sometimes,' she added with a pout. 'But that is the way it is with Greek men—the women of their own family must behave with so much circumspection, but they do not mind being friends with other women who behave differently.'

Megan laughed dryly. 'They're the same the whole world over,' she remarked. 'It's called the double standard.'

'English men are like that also?'

'If they think they can get away with it. English women mostly don't let them—not these days.'

Eleni shook her head. 'I think I would want to do as my husband wished. I would not like to argue.' The eyes beneath the fringe had taken on a sly look. 'You have met Theo?'

Something in her tone stirred Megan's suspicion; it did not seem like a coincidence that she should have mentioned Theo's name in almost the same sentence as the word 'husband'. 'He…flew over with us,' she responded with care.

'Ah—of course.' Eleni sighed wistfully, swinging her hair. 'I thought perhaps he might be still here.'

'He had to go back to England. Business,' Megan explained, her voice taut.

'Ah. He spends so much of his time in England.' Again that irritating movement with her hair. 'I wish he would be here more.'

Megan wasn't sure what to say. Was there something she didn't know about Eleni and Theo? She certainly wasn't going to ask—she wasn't especially interested anyway. It was just…she was a little annoyed, that was all—she would have liked to know if he was already spoken for. She might have decided not to let him kiss her.

CHAPTER FOUR

OVER the next few days several more members of the family descended upon them—as Dakis trenchantly remarked, they seemed to treat the villa as some kind of free hotel. Megan wondered frequently why he tolerated their presence at all, since it seemed to cause him so much annoyance. But she was soon driven to the conclusion that Theo had been right—he actually seemed to enjoy the frequent loud arguments and histrionics. She could only hope that it wouldn't have too damaging an effect on his blood pressure.

She also came to realise that she was going to earn every penny of the huge salary she was being paid. Dakis had been difficult enough when he had been in hospital in England, but here in his own home, where he was accustomed to having his every whim instantly obeyed, he was almost impossible.

Fortunately the Mediterranean diet—rich in fresh fruit and vegetables from his own farms and cooked in healthy olive oil—wasn't a problem, although she would have liked to be able to curb his taste for the sweet, sticky pastries he could consume by the plateful. And she wasn't too concerned about the amount of rich red wine he knocked back. It was his cigars that worried her; he had one alight almost as soon as he woke up in the morning, and virtually chain-smoked them through the day.

'How on earth can you enjoy those things, when you smoke them one after the other like that?' she demanded one day in weary exasperation. 'I thought the whole point of cigars was to savour them.'

'I do savour them,' he countered irascibly. 'I wouldn't smoke them if I didn't.'

'Well, don't light another one yet,' she warned. 'It's time for your exercise.'

He scowled impatiently. 'Huh! Sitting on that damn cycle, pedalling away…'

'You can have a change from the exercise bike today,' she conceded. 'Why don't you try the rowing machine?'

'That's just as bad,' he grumbled. 'I don't know what sadist invented those things, but I hope he's suffered as much as he's made everyone else suffer!'

'Ah, come on—stop grumbling. It's just for twenty minutes, and it doesn't have to be too strenuous. Just enough to get your muscles working nicely, like the doctor has said. And then I'll give you a massage.'

He muttered a bit more, but she just stood waiting, her arms folded, refusing to argue with him. Finally he gave in, reaching for his walking stick and levering himself awkwardly out of his wicker chair. 'You might at least help me up.'

'You can manage,' she insisted ruthlessly. 'You wouldn't want me to treat you like an invalid, would you?'

'You're a cruel woman,' he accused, his eyes glittering. 'I thought nurses were supposed to be kind and caring.'

She chuckled. 'You were the one who wanted me to come and work for you,' she reminded him.

'Huh! I must have been crazy!'

But it was with good humour that he finally allowed her to coax him along to the gymnasium on the ground floor next to the swimming pool. It was furnished with all the very latest computerised keep-fit equipment, but Megan doubted if it was used very often.

She had got into the habit of spending an hour in there every afternoon, while Dakis had his nap. She had never had to worry about fitness when she'd been hospital nursing—the job had kept her on her toes all day. But now, with just one patient to look after, she was afraid she might be in danger of getting lazy.

Nothing had been said about when—or even whether—Theo would be returning, and she had no intention of asking. But about two weeks after he had left, as she and Dakis strolled back out to the terrace after their morning's physiotherapy session, she was a little surprised to see him lounging on one of the wicker chairs with Sophia and Eleni.

She felt her heart give an odd little thud—but that was probably just because she was a little out of breath from the exertion, she excused herself swiftly. She was uncomfortably aware of him watching her as she walked towards him, those blue eyes lingering over the length of her slender legs with insolent appreciation. She returned him a look of icy disdain; it was true that she was wearing shorts, but until this moment she had thought of them as perfectly decent.

Eleni, she couldn't help but notice, was looking cool and demure in a pretty flower-sprigged dress of a delicate shade of pink, with a softly flared skirt that just brushed her knees. The picture of girlish charm, she mused acidly—if only she wouldn't simper and swing her hair around like that.

'Good morning.' Theo's tone held its customary hint of mockery for both Megan and his father. 'I hope you haven't been...exerting yourself too much?'

The old man chuckled. 'My nurse has been giving me

a massage,' he responded, a wicked glint in his eyes. 'Just the thing to get the blood pumping, as she keeps telling me.'

'I'm quite sure it does.' Those eyes once again lingered over her skimpy shorts.

'Goodness, that sounds terribly energetic!' Eleni exclaimed, gazing up ingenuously at Megan. 'Aren't you sweating?'

'Ladies don't sweat,' Theo reminded her, though his gaze was still on Megan. 'They merely glow.'

'And I'm glowing buckets,' Megan asserted, meeting that mocking gaze in defiant challenge.

That hard mouth curved into a smile of subtle sensuality that had a more alarming effect on her pulse than a whole morning in the gym. 'Have some orange juice,' he invited, reaching behind him to pull another of the wicker chairs up to the table. 'Papa?'

Dakis had already eased himself into another chair, leaning his walking stick against a flower-tub beside him. *'Efcharistó,'* he agreed with a nod.

Theo poured the juice from the tall jug on the table into two glasses. 'I gather you've actually managed to get my father to take some proper exercise,' he remarked as he handed Megan hers. 'I'm impressed.'

'He's cutting down on his cigars, as well,' she informed him coolly. 'Only six a day, and the first one not till after lunch.'

'Very good. How did you manage to achieve so much in so short a time?'

Dakis laughed softly, slanting his son a sly look. 'She has a very persuasive personality.'

'I'm sure she has.'

He hadn't stopped looking at her since she had walked out onto the terrace, those blue eyes conveying a mes-

sage that evoked disturbing memories of the night he
had shown up at her flat, and it was beginning to make
her feel uncomfortable. But with an effort of will she
made herself appear relaxed, lounging back in her chair,
one slim foot propped on the stone wall that surrounded
a flowerbed, sipping her orange juice.

'I wasn't expecting you back,' Dakis remarked to
Theo. 'Are you staying this time?'

'For a while. I thought perhaps I ought to…keep an
eye on things.'

Megan threw him a sardonic look, letting him know
that she was perfectly well aware that it was her—and
at this moment quite specifically her slender legs, toasted
to a light golden brown by the sun—that he was keeping
an eye on.

'Good! Well, in that case you can make yourself useful,' Dakis declared, apparently oblivious to any hidden
layers of meaning in the conversation. 'You can take a
trip over to Nicosia, and see what's happening about this
damned bottling plant they're supposed to be installing.
It's been nothing but delays and excuses! If I was fit
enough I'd go myself, but I'm not up to it yet.'

'Oh, Cousin Theo—can I come too?' Eleni put in excitedly. 'I'd love to go shopping in Nicosia.'

Dakis scowled. 'Shopping?' he grumbled impatiently.
'You don't need Theo to take you shopping. He's got
more important things to do.'

Eleni pouted, swinging her hair. 'Oh, but I must have
a new dress, and some shoes, and Cousin Theo always
knows just what's fashionable,' she argued, slanting a
coyly adoring look up at him from beneath her lashes.
'Please take me,' she begged prettily. 'I promise I won't
be in your way.'

Theo smiled down at her with a kind of lazy affection.

'You can come,' he agreed, his tone implying that there had been no need to make such a fuss about it.

Megan felt an odd little stab of pain in the region of her heart that she didn't care to examine too closely. The way he had smiled at Eleni, the way he had so readily agreed to take her with him to Nicosia, suggested that the chit had some grounds for her hints that there was something going on between them. She would never have expected him to fall for the wiles of a little *ingénue* like that—somehow she would have liked to think better of him.

Eleni turned to her, her mouth sweetly curved, her eyes conveying a smugness that was at striking odds with her display of artless naïvety. 'Why don't you come too, Megan?' she pleaded with a show of hollow enthusiasm. 'You'd love Nicosia.'

Megan took a moment to answer, her mind swiftly examining the proposition from every angle. She had no particular desire to spend the day in Theo's company—nor Eleni's, come to that. And she suspected that watching the two of them together would be even less delightful.

'No, thank you,' she responded, careful to keep all trace of her thoughts out of her voice. 'I want to make sure Dakis keeps to his programme for a few more days yet.'

'That's right,' Dakis put in, leaning over to pat her hand in a possessive gesture. 'Megan's supposed to be taking care of me—aren't you, *poulaki mou*? I can't have you gadding off, can I?'

Theo didn't miss the gesture, and his eyes hardened. 'I hope you're not making poor Megan work too hard, Papa?' he queried, a sardonic inflection in his voice.

'Not at all,' Dakis responded, his expression rather too saintly. 'Am I, my dear?'

'Of course not,' she purred, angry enough with Theo to go along with the old devil's game. 'You're the best.'

Theo rose abruptly from the table. 'Well, if you'll excuse me—if I'm going to Nicosia, I need to make a few phone calls first,' he announced, a hard edge in his voice. 'I'll be ready to leave in about half an hour, Eleni.'

'Oh, yes!' Eleni scrambled to her feet. 'I'll be ready—I'll meet you in the hall, yes?'

'Of course.' The smile he bestowed on her was warm as silk; the one he slid towards Megan had a snake-like quality. 'Goodbye, Nurse Taylor.'

'Goodbye,' she responded, her expression schooled into one of cool indifference.

He walked away, Eleni skipping along happily beside him. Megan watched them go, her mind a tangle of confused emotions. She had known—in spite of her resistance—that she was attracted to Theo. And it was understandable that she should be angry with him, after the way he had behaved towards her. What she hadn't expected was to feel jealous and hurt at seeing him with another woman.

Damn him! He was playing games, just as much as his father was, conveying messages with those incredible blue eyes that made her remember the fierce passion of his kiss, and the next minute appearing to encourage Eleni's immature coquettishness. No doubt being the object of such adolescent adoration appealed to his outsized ego, she reflected acidly—it was something he would never get from a grown woman.

Sophia, too, watched as the couple walked away, and

then sighed romantically, turning to Dakis to say something to him in Greek.

He laughed harshly. 'Hah! If you think he'd ever be fool enough to marry that silly little *kouneli* you're even stupider than I thought, Sophia,' he retorted. 'She couldn't keep him interested for five minutes!'

The woman's sour face twisted in annoyance, and, snapping something at him in Greek, she rose to her feet with a flounce and strode off in the direction of the kitchens—no doubt to aggravate the cook with petty demands about the evening meal, as she had done every day since she had arrived.

Dakis chuckled. 'That's put a flea in her ear!' he declared. 'Does she think I'm senile? That I can't see what she's up to? Well, if she and that blockish husband of hers think throwing her niece at my son will be a way into having a hand in the company, they're wasting their time.'

'Theo seems to like her,' Megan remarked carefully.

'Huh! If he marries her, I shall cut him off without a penny.'

Megan laughed, shaking her head. 'You know you won't do that. Besides, I doubt if it would bother him—he's rich enough in his own right. I'm afraid you're likely to find that if he wants to marry her there won't be very much you can do about it.'

The old man merely smiled enigmatically. 'Oh, I've a few more tricks up my sleeve just yet,' he assured her with a laugh. 'I told you—I'm used to getting my own way, and I'm too old to change now.'

She didn't see Theo for the rest of the day—he didn't return for dinner. Eleni was absent too—a fact which appeared to cause Sophia some satisfaction. Megan preferred not to consider the possible implications.

The next day followed the pattern that had become established over the past couple of weeks. After she had settled Dakis for his afternoon nap, she changed into a blue leotard, and went down to the gymnasium for her regular session. It was a large room, made to appear larger by the full-length mirrors that lined the walls. There were no windows, just two skylights set into the wood-panelled ceiling, but the temperature was kept pleasantly cool by the air-conditioning that hummed softly in the background.

She slipped one of her favourite rock-music tapes into the cassette deck, and as the pulsing rhythm filled the room she began her warm-up exercises, concentrating all her attention on the simple sequence of movements, watching her own reflection in the mirrors only to ensure she was doing them correctly, refusing to let herself conjure any disturbing images of blue eyes watching her, of a hard mouth smiling in insolent appreciation.

Once her muscles were well loosened she had a spell on the rowing machine, and then moved on to the row of weight-training equipment. There were ten pieces of apparatus, some of them looking more like something the Spanish Inquisition might have used than state-of-the-art, computerised fitness machines. Each one was designed to exercise a specific set of muscles using precisely counter-balanced loads, and soon she could feel the buzz of energy in her veins.

She was doing sit-ups on the slant-board, pumping vigorously to the rhythm of the loud rock music that was blasting out of the speakers on the wall, and didn't hear the door open. The first she realised that she wasn't alone was when she looked up to see Theo standing at her head.

'Good afternoon,' he greeted her, a sardonic inflection in his voice. 'It seems like hard work, keeping that tempting body in such delectable shape.'

She grunted as she pulled herself up for another abdominal crunch. 'I like to keep fit,' she retorted, refusing to let herself be needled.

'Fit for what?' He arched one dark eyebrow in mocking enquiry. 'I can't imagine you need to develop your stamina to keep up with my father.'

'You're disgusting.'

He laughed, soft and husky, low in his throat. 'Such fine indignation. Though I must admit I haven't quite made my mind up about you yet.' He moved, and before she realised what he was going to do he had swung one leg across the slant-board and was sitting on her thighs, trapping her. 'Unlike my dear cousin Giorgos—he harbours no doubts whatsoever.'

'I really don't give a damn what he thinks,' she retorted heatedly. It was impossible to maintain her dignity, lying there with her head at the lower end of the slant-board, forced to look up at him from such an awkward angle.

'Why should you?' One fingertip was tracing lazy circles across her stomach. 'He's no match for you. I, on the other hand, could be infinitely more dangerous—as I warned you. But you chose to take your chance. You only have yourself to blame for the consequences.'

Slowly, deliberately, he was letting that fingertip trace a wider circle, until it brushed against the soft underside of her breasts. His eyes were holding hers, challenging her to protest, as she struggled to distance herself from the treacherous response he was arousing. But beneath the clinging Lycra jersey of her leotard her breasts were achingly warm, her tender nipples puckering to taut buds, tingling with anticipation.

'What about...Eleni?' she demanded, her voice as ragged as her breathing.

'Ah, yes—sweet little Eleni.' His fingertip was trailing in a figure-of-eight now over the firm swell of her breasts. 'My virgin bride, if Cousin Sophia has her way. I confess the idea has its merits. Not that virgins are particularly to my taste. I tend to like my women like my wine—a little more mature, with that little extra...something to intrigue the palate.'

That lazy fingertip was still circling over her breasts, closer and tantalisingly closer to the ripened peaks that now showed so pertly and invitingly beneath the taut blue Lycra. Part of her hated him for treating her like this, but part of her knew that she only had to tell him to stop and he would. But, to her shame, she didn't want him to stop. She wanted him to go on—though he was stripping away every inch of her self-respect.

And then his palm brushed almost idly across her nipple, and her breath caught suddenly in her throat as a hot shaft of electricity sizzled through her. He laughed softly, cupping and caressing each exquisitely aching breast as her spine curved into a quivering arc to crush them into his hands.

Her head tipped back, and some kind of inarticulate sound—half of protest, half of pleading—escaped from her throat as he bent over her, his mouth hot on the vulnerable curve of her throat, finding the tiny spot behind the lobe of her ear, scalding a line of kisses down into the sensitive hollow of her shoulder.

He had been taunting her, arousing her with that devastating expertise while keeping himself almost coolly detached, but now she sensed that iron control beginning to crack. With some fierce, muttered imprecation in Greek, his hands tensed, those tantalising caresses becoming almost rough, and she gasped as he pinched at her tender nipples, rolling them between his fingers, torturing her with a sharp pleasure as she exalted in the recognition of her own power to tip him over the edge.

'Damn you,' he grated savagely, his hot breath scalding her cheek. 'Are you from heaven or from hell? You provoke me with your sharp tongue, and taunt me with those cool smiles, making me want you, making me feel as if I'll never know any peace until I've had you...'

His head bent over hers again to claim her mouth in a kiss of fierce intensity, and her lips parted in helpless surrender, offering him no resistance as his tongue swept deep into every sweet, secret corner in a flagrantly sensual invasion that ignited the fires of her response. He dragged one strap of her leotard down over the curve of her shoulder, uncovering her naked breast beneath his caressing hands, and his body was heavy on hers, forcing her thighs apart, moving against her so that it was almost as if they were already making love...

'Theo...?'

The sound of Eleni's voice in the passage outside broke them abruptly apart. Muttering a curse, he slid swiftly over to perch casually on one of the other machines as Megan straightened her leotard, far too conscious of the vivid scarlet blush in her cheeks—hopefully Eleni would assume it was from the exercise. By the time the door opened she was once again crunching her stomach muscles in rhythmic sit-ups as Theo sat idly watching her.

'Oh... Here you are.' Eleni sounded a little uncertain,

clearly unhappy at finding him with Megan. 'Aunt Sophia sent me to find you.'

'What does she want?'

'I...don't know. Something to do with dinner, I think.'

'Why on earth does she need me to sort out anything to do with dinner?' he protested in good-natured exasperation. 'Okay, *agape mou*, I'm coming. I'll see you later,' he added softly to Megan; she wasn't sure if it was only her imagination that detected a hint of promise—or warning.

Megan stood in front of the mirror in her bedroom, gazing at her own familiar reflection, feeling as if she was looking at a stranger. It wasn't just the sun-kissed sheen of her skin, glowing bronze against the dainty white lace of her underwear, nor the toned slenderness of her long legs. It was as if she had been branded everywhere that Theo had touched her, marked by his possession.

His words were still echoing in her brain—*I'll never know any peace until I've had you...* She drew in a long, shuddering breath, closing her eyes, but she couldn't shut out the images those words conjured. She would know no peace either; her body ached with a hunger that only his could assuage.

But for her there would be no peace afterwards—perhaps no peace ever again. Because she knew that if she surrendered he would take her only to ease that primitive physical need—nothing more. And for her that would never be enough.

This afternoon, when Eleni had walked into the gym, he had been able to turn off the heat in a fraction of a second, to smile as if nothing had happened—while she had felt a bitter humiliation, knowing that he could only treat her with such casual dismissiveness if he didn't care about her at all.

Fool! she castigated herself, opening her eyes to stare again at her own image in the mirror. Did you ever think he would? He uses women. You've seen what they say about him in the papers. Did you think it wasn't true? Women much more beautiful than you. It's all just a game to him, adding up how many he can score. He probably will marry Eleni, because she'll be sweet and biddable, willing to stay at home and have his babies, and not make a fuss when he's unfaithful to her—as he will be, over and over again. And any woman stupid enough to let herself fall in love with him will get exactly what she deserves!

Impatiently she brushed a tear from her cheek with the back of her hand, smudging the mascara she had already applied. Dabbing it away with a tissue, she picked up the wand and carefully repaired the damage. That was how it would be, she vowed fiercely—she would repair the damage that had already been done to her self-respect, and she wouldn't let it happen again. And she certainly wouldn't let herself fall in love with him.

Slipping into her dress and zipping it up, she paused to examine her reflection in the mirror again, frowning slightly. Was this dress a mistake? Since Giorgos and Sophia's arrival, dinner had been quite a formal affair—though Dakis, in his usual spirit of mischievous defiance, often wore casual clothes, sometimes even shorts. She usually chose something fairly simple—she didn't own anything that wouldn't look out of place beside the expensive, designer-label outfits the women of the family generally wore.

The dress was one of Cathy's—she had absolutely

insisted she should bring it with her. It was red—correction, it was a vibrant shade of scarlet—the sort of colour that smacked you right between the eyes. Fortunately, since she was a little slimmer than Cathy, the deeply plunging neckline wasn't *too* shocking, but since she was also several inches taller the skirt was extremely short. She was certainly going to raise a few eyebrows tonight!

Well, so what? she challenged her reflection. They all thought she was some scheming little gold-digger anyway—she might as well live up to their nasty expectations. With a defiant little shrug of her shoulders, she turned away from the mirror, and, drawing in a long, deep breath, she steeled herself to face the evening ahead.

She could hear voices coming from the main sitting room as she walked down the stairs—a lot of voices. A small frown creased her brow. No one had mentioned that there were going to be additional guests for dinner.

She had almost reached the foot of the stairs when the door opened, and Sophia swept out into the hall—Sophia *á la grande dame*, in a full length evening gown of black moiré satin that rustled as she walked, a strikingly ugly necklace of dusty diamonds dangling around her thin neck. She stopped abruptly when she saw Megan, her sharp little eyes conveying very clearly her opinion of the scarlet dress.

'Did Eleni not tell you that we are tonight dressing for dinner?' she demanded, glaring at her down her haughty nose. 'We have the honour of entertaining her parents.'

Megan felt her cheeks flush slightly. 'No, she didn't mention it.' A deliberate omission? Almost certainly—

it wouldn't have been the sort of thing she would have forgotten. So the little kitten had claws after all.

'You must go and change at once,' Sophia commanded, waving her hand. 'And please hurry—already you keep us waiting.'

Megan gave her an acid smile. 'Oh, dear—I *am* sorry. Perhaps I'd better just stay as I am, then—I'm sure no one will mind.' And, with a proud lift of her head, she sashayed across the hall to the main sitting room, her high-heeled gold sandals—also borrowed from Cathy—making her hips sway with a provocative rhythm.

But on the threshold she hesitated, her defiant spirit wavering slightly. The conversation stopped dead, and every eye in the room turned to stare. It had been no understatement that they were dressing for dinner—they looked as if they were about to set off for the opera. The men all wore formal black dinner-jackets, and the women, like Sophia, were in satin or silk, in dark, sophisticated colours, and dripping with enough jewels to fill a bank vault.

She could feel a hot blush of pink rising to her cheeks, and the temptation to turn and run was almost overwhelming. And then she saw Theo across the room, those blue eyes coolly watching her, their expression unreadable.

And clinging to his side like a limpet was Eleni, her natural prettiness somewhat overwhelmed by a dress of doll-pink taffeta laden with ruffles around the low neckline and wide hem. She had rather inadvisedly added a diamanté slide to her hair, which clashed badly with the debutante pearls around her throat, and she had been a little heavy-handed with the blue eye-shadow, so that it looked as if a couple of moths had landed on her eyelids.

The smile she slanted towards Megan glinted with smug satisfaction at the success of her petty trick.

It was Dakis who came to her rescue, appearing at her side, a mischievous twinkle in his eyes as he slipped his arm through hers. 'Ah, there you are, my dear. And looking as lovely as a rose.'

She smiled up at him with gratitude. 'I didn't know you were having guests for dinner,' she murmured. 'Maybe it would have been better if I hadn't come down.'

'Nonsense! What would I do without your pretty face to cheer me up? Now, you must meet Eleni's parents. Her father's a prefect, you know—a most important personage indeed, as he makes sure we all understand! I have told them *all* about you.'

'I just bet you have,' Megan murmured wryly. '*What* have you told them?'

He chuckled. 'Why, that you are my private nurse, of course—and that you are taking very *special* care of me.'

'That's what I was afraid of.'

'Ah, it is just a little game,' he soothed. 'What is the English expression for it? To put the cat amidst the pigeons, yes? So! Let us ruffle a few pigeon-feathers. It will serve them right, don't you think?'

Megan had to acknowledge that he had a point. They were all so concerned about their stupid inheritance that they were ready to jump to all sorts of conclusions about her, on the flimsiest of evidence. Why not have a bit of fun at their expense by acting up to their nasty, narrow-minded prejudices and making fools of them?

And then there was Theo, she mused tautly—he was the worst of all of them, by a long chalk. From beneath her lashes, she slanted another covert glance across the room. She had to admit he looked good in a dinner-jacket. It was immaculately cut, but he wore it with a casual panache which subtly underplayed its formality, the jacket loosely open, one hand in the pocket of his black trousers. So arrogant, so supremely sure of himself...

'Okay,' she decided, smiling brightly up at Dakis. 'Let's really give them something to be scandalised about.'

Flirtatious giggles and fluttering of eyelashes were not skills she had ever seen the need to cultivate, but it was quite remarkable how effectively she could produce them when she wanted to. Dakis laughed, and slapped her lightly on the bottom, to which she protested with a pout, thoroughly enjoying the frisson of disapproval that ran through the assembled company.

Dakis was leaning quite heavily on her arm as they crossed the room—he was using a slim ebony cane tonight instead of his much sturdier tripod-footed walking stick. Still, there was no harm in a little vanity, she acknowledged with a private smile. He looked almost as elegant as his son in his expensively tailored dinner-jacket—once he must have been almost as handsome.

The group they joined included Giorgos and his battleaxe wife, but very much at centre-stage was a tall, extremely distinguished-looking man, with even more of an air of self-importance than Giorgos. The woman at his side was undoubtedly Eleni's mother—obviously once beautiful, a lifelong habit of petulance had etched ugly lines around her mouth and eyes, so that she looked as if she was permanently sucking on a lemon.

'Ah, Dimitrios—how do you do?' Dakis greeted his guest with unaccustomed warmth. 'And Ekaterina! How breathtakingly lovely you look tonight.'

Eyes like black ice glittered at him; Megan was reminded of the ancient myth of Medusa, who could turn a man to stone with one look.

But Dakis was thoroughly enjoying himself. 'Now, my dear, allow me to introduce you,' he went on, patting Megan's hand. 'This is Eleni's mother and father. And this is my little nurse, who has devoted herself to taking care of me.'

Megan found herself the subject of a high-nosed stare, as if she were something the cat had left on the carpet. And then they simply continued the conversation they had been having with Giorgos, ignoring Megan's presence as if she weren't even there.

Indignation bubbled up inside her—how *dared* they treat her so rudely? They didn't even know her! Well, they would get full measure tonight—she was going to enjoy herself. Turning to Dakis and leaning close to him, she brushed an imaginary speck of dust from the immaculate collar of his dinner-jacket.

'Daki, sweetie, could I have just a *wee* glass of wine?' she purred coquettishly. 'I promise I won't get tipsy.'

'You can have whatever you want!' he declared, his voice booming. 'Vlamis—two glasses of wine,' he added to the manservant who was circulating discreetly among the guests with a silver tray.

Theo was still talking quietly to Eleni—but across the room his eyes met Megan's, and she could see the glint of cold hostility in them. So he didn't appreciate her little performance? Laughing merrily, she tossed back her hair, letting the yellow-blonde curls catch the light. Let him think whatever he damn well liked!

Suddenly she became aware of a general movement in the room. Eleni's father had stepped forward, and cleared his throat. It seemed that some kind of speech was expected, and when he began to speak—in

Greek—there were smiles and nods of approval. Megan was about to whisper to Dakis to ask what he was saying, but suddenly it became all too crystal-clear.

Everyone had turned to Theo and Eleni, raising their glasses to drink a toast. And for the first time Megan noticed the large solitaire diamond ring winking on the third finger of Eleni's left hand.

CHAPTER FIVE

'SHALL we go in to dinner, my dear?'

Megan blinked as Dakis spoke to her, struggling to conceal her reaction to the sudden shock of finding out about Theo's engagement. A dozen emotions were swirling in her brain—the strongest of which was anger. What sort of game was he playing? Kissing her the way he had, when just hours later he'd been planning to announce his engagement to the simpering little miss at his side...

'Of course.' She felt as if her smile had been set in place with superglue, but, drawing in a deep, steadying breath, she took Dakis's proffered arm to walk through the wide double doors that had been folded back, leading into the dining room.

It was clear that Sophia, with her usual talent for taking over, had decided that it was to be a spectacularly grand occasion. The long table had been fully extended to seat all the guests, and was laden with all the best glass and silverware, which sparkled in the light of half a dozen candelabra which had been lit along the table's length.

'How cosy!' remarked Dakis with sardonic humour. 'Come along, *poulaki mou*, you'll sit next to me, of course.'

But as they moved towards the head of the table Sophia planted herself in their way, fixing Megan with a glare fierce enough to stop a charging rhinoceros in its tracks. 'No, no,' she objected, pointing with one scrawny finger to a seat near the foot of the table. 'You sit there.'

'*Sakhlamares!*' Dakis barked, dismissing her with a wave of his hand. 'Megan will sit where *I* want her to sit. Go away, you silly woman, and stop bothering me.'

For one unpleasant moment it looked as if Sophia might argue—but then her ingrained conservatism, which would not permit her to disobey the head of the family, surfaced, and, meekly bowing her head, she stepped out of their way. But the look she slanted towards Megan from her narrowed black eyes would have stripped paint.

The disruption to the defined order of precedence caused some confusion in the seating arrangements, and there was a good deal of shuffling until everyone was settled. Then Megan glanced up—and found that she was seated directly across the table from Theo and his new fiancée.

He lifted his glass, those deep blue eyes regarding her with lazy mockery as he silently toasted her, taking a sip of his wine. To her chagrin, she felt a betraying blush of pink rise to her cheeks. Damn him! If only she could match his sang-froid, she thought acidly—she would have liked to be able to smile at him with cool formality, to congratulate him on his engagement, but she couldn't trust herself to speak.

And what about Eleni? She was in her element, the centre of attention, all coy sweetness, swinging her hair around as she deliberately let the light from the nearest candles spark fire into the huge diamond on her left hand. Did she have any idea what sort of man she was going to marry? But then maybe she didn't care—maybe the money and status of being his wife would be enough

for her. Leaving him free to pursue his...pleasures else-
where.

Well, if he thought he was going to lure Megan Taylor
into that sort of arrangement, he was going to have to
think again, she vowed resolutely. She couldn't deny the
powerful tug of physical attraction she felt towards him,
but that didn't mean she had to give in to the temptation.
She was twenty-nine years old, for goodness' sake—she
had held a highly responsible job in charge of a busy
operating theatre for two years, managing arrogant consultants and pushy young medical students with ease.
She ought to know a thing or two about handling men.
Admittedly there were few quite like Theo Nikolaides
around, but behind that air of cool self-assurance he
couldn't be that much different from any of the others.

But as she risked another cautious glance across the
table she found him still watching her, those deep blue
eyes glinting as he held her captive with their mesmeric
gaze. Her heartbeat began to race, making it difficult to
breathe, and she could feel her body responding as if he
was touching her, her breasts achingly ripe, the taut
peaks clearly contoured by the sheer silky fabric of her
dress.

A hot tinge of pink coloured her cheeks as she struggled to control her helpless reaction, but he was far too
perceptive not to notice those betraying signals. His hard
mouth curved into a slow smile, taunting her silently
with the evidence that just by looking at her like that he
could throw her into an emotional turmoil.

Somehow she managed to drag her eyes away, and
turned her attention to the colourful plate of choriátiki
salad and melting halloumi cheese in front of her. Dakis
had an excellent cook, and most evenings she had been
hungry enough to do full justice to his artistry, but to-

night her appetite seemed to have evaporated, and she could only pick at her food.

'You are feeling unwell, *poulaki mou*?' Dakis murmured, leaning close to her.

She slanted him a swift smile, shaking her head. 'I think Sophia's given me the evil eye,' she returned lightly.

'Hah! That one! Do not let her bother you, my little kitten—she would turn the milk sour fresh from the goat! Remember our little game? That is your way to have your revenge, yes? Here, you like the stuffed olives?' He selected one from his own plate, and held it out to her. 'They are good, yes?'

From beneath her lashes, she saw that Theo was again watching her with his father, a small frown of anger creased between his brows. Some foolish part of her wanted him not to think badly of her, but her defiant heart rebelled against such wimpishness. Let him think whatever he damn well liked!

'Of course I like olives,' she purred, turning her fine grey eyes to Dakis. 'I love them!'

'*Endaksi!*' He chuckled, popping it into her mouth. 'We will make a Cypriot of her yet, eh, Theo?'

His son smiled, that slow, taunting smile, as if to remind her of the danger she was courting. 'No doubt,' he agreed, lifting his wineglass to his lips in a mocking toast.

She returned him a glittering smile, and turned back to Dakis as he offered her a refill for her own wineglass, which she was a little surprised to find was already empty. She was going to have to be more careful to watch how much she had to drink, she reminded herself judiciously; the dark wine of Cyprus was a dangerous brew—velvet-smooth on the tongue, but with a bite that could make your head spin.

The salad was followed by a delicious chicken soup, delicately flavoured with lemon, and then the most tender lamb, marinated in wine and coriander, and served with a light pilaf of crushed wheat. By the time the sweet dessert of baklava—steeped in aromatic honey from the villa's own gardens—had been replaced by tiny cups of the fierce Turkish coffee that was so popular, Megan was beginning to feel as though she had been put through a wringer and hung out to dry. She would never have believed it possible, but the sheer effort of maintaining her role in the game, pretending to flirt with Dakis while ignoring Theo and his mocking eyes, was more exhausting than a ten-hour shift with a full operating schedule.

But at last Dakis pushed away his empty coffee-cup, and yawned widely. 'Well, it's been a delightful evening, but I'm afraid that at my age I no longer have the capacity for late nights. So if you will excuse us...' the smile he bestowed on the polite company around the table wickedly invited them to draw their own conclusions '..my nurse will put me to bed. My dear?'

He held out his arm to her, and with a show of effusive concern she helped him to his feet. In fact the concern was partly genuine—she could tell by the difficulty he had in moving that he was indeed very tired. As she helped him to the door, she could feel many pairs of eyes watching her, boring into her back like knives, but she forced herself to resist the temptation to look back. The comments, held in check until the door closed, instantly erupted in a babble of Greek that she was glad she couldn't understand.

Dakis laughed wickedly. 'Well, that was fun,' he declared. 'Don't you think?'

'Not exactly,' Megan responded dryly.

'Why not?' The dark eyes that slanted towards her were narrowed and shrewd; had he guessed that she wasn't exactly overjoyed at the announcement of his son's engagement?

'I'm…afraid I'm not very popular with Eleni's family,' she temporised cautiously.

He gave a sharp bark of laughter. 'Of course not! Just when they think they've outmanoeuvred me, you come along and they can see all their neat little plans going up in smoke.'

'I don't see why they should be so worried about it,' she protested. 'Even if they swallowed all that silly nonsense about me being some kind of gold-digger, I'm not that much of a threat to them.'

'Ah, but if they thought I was going to *marry* you…'

Megan stared at him, startled. 'You old devil! Don't you think you're taking this all a bit too far?'

'Not at all. It's simply the logical conclusion.'

'Well, I hope you don't think you're going to talk me into going through with it for real!' she warned him firmly. 'A little play-acting is one thing, but I definitely draw the line there!'

'Don't worry,' he assured her, patting her hand. 'I'm simply calling my son's bluff.'

'His bluff?'

'This silly engagement nonsense,' he responded impatiently. 'He has no more intention of marrying that empty-headed little ninny than flying to the moon.'

Megan felt her heart give a sharp thud. 'You…don't think so?'

'Of course he hasn't. He'd be bored stupid inside of a week, and he knows it.'

Except that he had no intention of restricting himself to just one woman, she reflected bitterly. He had already made that perfectly clear.

Megan closed the door of her room, leaning back against it with a sigh and closing her eyes. She wanted nothing more than the oblivion of sleep, but she had a feeling it was going to be difficult to find tonight—there was too much going on inside her head. Perhaps a nice warm shower would help her relax a little, she mused, unzipping her dress and stepping out of it.

It still didn't seem quite right to just leave it on the chair for the maid to collect in the morning. The next time she saw it, it would be beautifully laundered and ironed, hung on a hanger in her wardrobe. It was the sort of service that Eleni no doubt took as her due, but she still found it a little uncomfortable.

Which was just one of the reasons why Eleni would be exactly the sort of girl Theo would marry, she reflected dryly—she had been raised to this kind of life; she knew how the very rich were supposed to behave. Plus, she had the advantage of political clout, through her father—she wasn't precisely sure what a prefect was, but she guessed it was some kind of regional mayor.

While she herself probably wouldn't even make the grade as a bona-fide mistress—no doubt one of his elegant London girlfriends was already lined up for that role. She was just a convenient source of amusement while he was here in Cyprus—reasonably attractive, even if somewhat lacking the level of sophistication he was used to, but sharp enough to add a certain piquancy to the physical pleasures he could coax so expertly from her body.

Her cheeks flushed a fevered red at the memory of just *how* expertly he had coaxed those pleasures from her. She had never known anything quite like it. Even in the best days with Jeremy, early in their relationship when he had still been willing to make an effort to satisfy her, there had never been that sort of...sizzle. And in the end—for far longer than she had really been willing to admit—he had taken her for granted, and their relationship had dwindled into a kind of routine as they had both put the greater part of their energies into their careers.

But Theo seemed able to awaken some part of her that she had never even known existed—something as old as Eve. Making love with him would be the most incredible experience, something beyond her power even to imagine. Something she would never be so close to again...

She drew in a sharp breath, shaking her head to dispel that treacherous train of thought. Theo Nikolaides was going to marry his cousin Eleni. And, though she might be quite sure he was entering into the alliance out of pure self-interest in which love played no part, she could be equally sure that all he was offering her was a passing episode of sexual pleasure which he would terminate whenever it suited him.

And what's more, she reminded herself briskly, he thinks you're the sort of cheap little hussy who'd throw herself at a man damned nearly old enough to be her grandfather! Come on—you have far too much self-respect to let yourself get involved in something like that.

Quickly she stripped off her underwear and put it with

the dress, and then stepped into the small but luxurious *en-suite* bathroom. The shower gushed out a welcoming flow of warm water, and she stepped beneath it, smoothing a generous slick of creamy shower-gel over her skin and letting the soapy rivulets trickle down over her slender contours like a waterfall.

But some traitorous part of her mind still held onto the memory of the way Theo had kissed her, the way his hands had caressed her body, the way those deep blue eyes had seemed to control her very will.

The images were so vividly real that she almost felt as if he was watching her now as she stood naked beneath the shower, insolently appreciating every inch as if she were putting on some kind of private floor-show exclusively for him…dancing to a sultry music that was playing in her brain, moving her body to turn the provocative curve of her shoulder, letting him catch a tantalising glimpse of one creamy breast delicately tipped with pink, stroking her hands down over her smooth thighs… She knew that it was dangerous to let herself indulge such fantasies, but she didn't seem able to stop them.

She stayed under the water for a very long time, letting it wash away all the tension, all the ragged emotions that had been jangling her nerves. By the time she climbed out of the shower, and wrapped herself up in one of the huge, fluffy bath-towels that appeared freshly each morning, she felt warm and lazily relaxed, almost ready for sleep.

The maid had laid her cheap white broderie anglaise nightdress out on the bed, arranging it as carefully as if it had been of the finest silk. With a wide yawn Megan slipped it over her head, letting the towel fall to the floor so that she could carefully dry her feet. When she had finished, she put the towel back in the bathroom, and went to draw the curtains over the long windows that led out onto the balcony.

But instead the night lured her outside. The air was warm and soft, perfumed with jasmine and thyme, and the only sound was the slow, rhythmic whisper of the sea. She drew in a long, deep breath, gazing out over the velvet darkness of the water. The moon had laid down a track of silver, like a path of diamonds that seemed to lead all the way to heaven.

But there was no easy path to heaven, she reminded herself with a wistful sigh. It was just an illusion—if she tried to walk on it, she would sink into the dark, drowning waves...

A soft sound behind her startled her, and she turned her head as Theo slid open the French windows of the room next to hers, and stepped out onto the balcony beside her. 'Good evening,' he murmured, that customary inflection of mockery in his voice.

'How...how did you get here?' she protested stupidly.

'The back stairs from behind the gymnasium lead up to the end of the passage, and this room is empty— Ah...in need of some minor repairs, I believe. Hence I can pass through it whenever I wish. And since your room is at the corner of the wing there is no one on the other side. Convenient, don't you think?'

'You...arranged it like that,' she accused, her voice a little unsteady.

'Of course.' He was moving slowly towards her, his eyes holding her prisoner with their mesmeric blue gaze. 'I don't choose to let the whole household know my movements. Particularly at night.'

'You don't think they'd be likely to guess?' she threw back at him, struggling to control the agitated beating of her heart. 'I'm quite sure you've done this kind of thing before.'

He smiled indolently. 'Several times. And if they speculate—so what?' He shrugged in a gesture of casual unconcern. 'At least I make a semblance of discretion—that is all that is required.'

He was close to her now, so close that she could breathe the evocative musky scent of his skin. He was still wearing the pin-tucked white shirt he had had on earlier, but now it was unfastened at the throat, his silk bow-tie hanging loose beneath the collar, the pristine cuffs turned back over his strong wrists.

A little belatedly Megan remembered that she was wearing only her thin cotton nightdress. Instinctively she wrapped her arms around her body, taking a step back—to find herself trapped against the rail of the balcony. Her eyes widened as he came closer still, until she was gazing up at him, and he seemed to fill her whole horizon.

'Running scared?' he taunted softly. 'You told me when we first met that you weren't afraid of me. You have learned to be a little wiser. Unfortunately, you have left it rather too late.' Those cool eyes slid down over her, lazily mocking. 'That's a very fetching nightgown. Sweet and virginal—something of a change from the scarlet woman you paraded before us at dinner. But I like the contrast—it...intrigues me.'

Cornered, she glared up at him in angry defiance, refusing to let him see that she was afraid of him. 'Oh, yes—speaking of virgins,' she countered, not quite able to keep her voice as steady as she would have liked, 'you didn't tell me you were going to marry Eleni.'

'Didn't I?'

'You know you didn't. You implied...'

'That my tastes run to riper fruits. Indeed they do.' He put out his hand, sliding one finger beneath her chin, tilting it up to study her face in the moonlight. 'I prefer a woman who can match my appetites, who knows how to respond when I kiss her, whose body melts beneath my caresses like warm honey. A woman whose breasts are warm and round and inviting, firm beneath my hand…'

He was holding her captive with that mesmerising blue gaze as slowly, slowly he let his fingertip trail down the length of her throat…and on, tracing the dainty picot edging of her nightdress, brushing lightly over her soft skin, still silky and fragrant from her shower…down into the shadowy valley between her breasts.

'Warm…and round…and inviting…' His voice was low and husky, weaving a sensual spell around her, subduing her will. 'Like sun-ripened peaches, rich and succulent, waiting to be plucked…'

She drew in a long, ragged breath, helpless to stop him as he brushed one strap of the nightdress down over the curve of her shoulder, letting it fall, uncovering the naked roundness of one firm breast, a paler cream against the gold of her tan, the tender pink nipple hardening into a taut bud beneath the raw hunger of his gaze.

'*Omorfi*… Beautiful,' he growled, that hard mouth curving slowly into a smile of satisfaction.

He touched his fingertip to the pert peak, sending sizzling sparks through every nerve-fibre in her body. She closed her eyes, breathing out slowly between her teeth, all her senses focused on that exquisite point of contact as his fingertip circled lazily around the flushed aureole.

'Do you want me to stop?' he queried, his voice laced with cool mockery. 'You only have to say the word…

But we both know you won't, don't we? This is what you want—this is what you need…'

With a sudden ruthlessness he dragged her into his arms, his hand crushing her breast beneath the delicious abrasion of his palm as his mouth descended on hers with an almost savage intensity, parting her lips with a crushing force so that his hot tongue could plunder the sweetest depths within.

Her small whimper of protest turned into a low moan of pleasure as her head tipped dizzily back and she let him curve her against the hard length of his body, her breathing ragged and her blood swirling like a fever through her veins.

'Yes,' he whispered fiercely. 'This is how I want you—forced to surrender to your own unquenchable hunger, to offer me all the pleasures of your sweet, tender flesh…'

His mouth came down to claim hers again with a searing heat, overcoming her will to resist him. He was plundering ruthlessly every deep, secret corner of her mouth, and she found herself kissing him back, the irresistible pull of her senses forcing her to yield beneath that invasion.

She knew she shouldn't be letting this happen, but she didn't know how to control her response, every quiver of her body betraying how truly he had spoken. His hand was on her naked breast, moulding and caressing the ripe, aching flesh, his clever fingers teasing the tender peak into a sizzling sensitivity, darting white fire into her brain.

She was barely aware that he had eased her down onto the canvas sun-lounger. His hands were tangled in her hair, and his hot mouth was tracing a scalding path of kisses across her trembling eyelids, finding the tumultuous pulse beneath her temple, swirling into the delicate shell of her ear.

'*Pekhnidi mou,*' he murmured, huskily soft. 'My pretty little plaything…'

His words pierced the mists that were swirling in her brain, dragging her back to the bitter recollection of the announcement that had been made earlier in the evening. 'No,' she protested raggedly. 'I'm not your plaything.'

'Oh, yes, you are,' he asserted, a note of certainty in his voice. 'Whenever I want you. You can fight it all you want, but you won't win—the temptation is much too strong for you.'

And with ruthless expertise he proceeded to demonstrate the truth of his claim, capturing her wrists as she tried to struggle against him and pinning them back above her head, laughingly ignoring her vicious invective as his mouth brushed over hers, warm and enticing, his languorous tongue tracing the soft contours of her lips, beguiling her senses, undermining her will to resist him.

His hand moved again to the firm swell of her breast, and she felt herself responding helplessly to his touch, a slow, languid warmth spreading through her veins. His kisses were tracing a scalding path down the long, sensitive column of her throat, and on over the ripe, naked curves, his hot tongue swirling around the taut pink peak of her nipple, lapping at it, teasing it with his hard white teeth as her spine curled into a quivering arch beneath him, offering herself to him in wanton invitation.

A low, shuddering sigh escaped her lips as at last he took the sweet, dainty bud into his mouth, and began to suckle it with a deep, hungry rhythm that pulsed through her heated blood, melting her brain. She was surrendering without thought or reason to his expert caresses, lost in the dark swirl of erotic pleasure that was sweeping her away...

But abruptly he lifted his head, his blue eyes mocking her startled grey ones. 'So,' he taunted, an edge of sardonic humour in his soft voice. 'Time for the truth now, don't you think?'

'The...truth?'

'Unless you really want me to believe that you're so cheap, so totally lacking in any kind of moral standards, that you would be prepared to have an affair with both father and son.'

'I...' She stared up at him, her addled brain struggling to find some way out of the trap he had so neatly set for her.

He laughed, shaking his head. 'I thought not. I'm afraid my dear papa isn't quite as clever as he thinks he is. You may be able to fool poor old Giorgos, but you don't fool me.'

'I *did* fool you,' she countered, finding her voice in bitter triumph. 'You certainly believed it to begin with.'

'Oh, I admit I was a little distracted at first by those sexy black silk stockings,' he acknowledged, his mouth curving into a smile of reminiscence. 'They made it a little...difficult to think straight. But I've had time to watch you with him now. You're really not a very good actress, you know—you keep forgetting your role.'

She sat up, her cheeks flushing a heated red as she pulled up the strap of her nightgown, the cotton rough against her sensitised flesh. 'Yes, well... It was just a game,' she admitted thickly. 'It was Dakis's idea. All the family were making it so obvious that they could hardly wait to get their hands on his money, he thought it would be fun to rile them up a bit.'

'Is that so?' There was a glint of amusement in his

eyes. 'And maybe he was hoping it would bring me into line as well?'

'That…did enter into it,' she conceded tautly.

'I thought so. The old fool—he doesn't give up, does he?' There was that same note of pride and affection in his voice when he spoke of his father, as when Dakis spoke of him. But he was still watching her, his eyes narrowed with suspicion. 'And what's in it for you?'

'Me?' She shrugged her slim shoulders, struggling for some semblance of composure. 'Oh, just…a couple of months in the sun, with better wages than I could get anywhere at home.'

Suddenly she was uncomfortably aware that there was a little more to it than that. It had something to do with Theo, something that had hooked her from their very first, fleeting encounter in the sluice; something that had lured her in, though she had known it was foolish to let herself succumb to the temptation.

'Is that all?' He lifted his hand to her cheek, the pad of his thumb tracing the soft contours of her lips, which were still warm and aching from his kisses. 'No more than that?'

'Of…course not!' she insisted raggedly. 'What else could there be?'

'You tell me,' he responded, his eyes far too perceptive. 'Maybe…you found you liked it, the first time I kissed you? Maybe, like me, you couldn't help wondering what the possibilities might be…?'

She drew in a long, deep breath, struggling to resist the spell he was weaving around her. Did he really expect her to admit that it had been that powerful tug of physical attraction—though she had done all she could to deny it—that had made it inevitable from the beginning that she would accept Dakis's offer?

'I think you have a problem with your ego,' she responded, injecting a note of frosty dignity into her voice. 'Not *every* woman in the world finds you irresistible, you know.' She brushed his hand away, and stood up. 'Now, if you'll excuse me—it's very late, and I'm tired. Goodnight.'

He arched one dark eyebrow, mocking her flimsy pretence of indifference, but he made no attempt to detain her. 'Goodnight,' he replied, rising easily to his feet, as cool as if nothing of the last few minutes had taken place. 'I'll see you in the morning.' And he disappeared the same way he had arrived, through the empty room next to hers.

Megan stood at the open patio door, her hand resting on the frame to steady herself—her bones still felt as if they were made of jelly. And he had just walked away! Not that she had wanted him to stay, of course—it was just that…now she was left with even more doubts. Had he really been attracted to her at all? Or had it all been a pretence to make her confess the truth about her 'relationship'—or rather the absence of it—with his father?

Damn him! He had deployed that powerful physical magnetism like a weapon, luring her into betraying just how vulnerable she was—and then he had left her standing here, feeling like a complete fool. Impatiently she dashed a hand across her eyes, annoyed at finding them wet with tears. On top of everything else, she had let him make her cry.

CHAPTER SIX

MEGAN slept badly, troubled by dreams she didn't want to remember in the morning. But, though it was late when she woke, she didn't rush to get dressed—she was in no particular hurry to face Theo, or to see the simpering Eleni flashing her engagement ring around.

But there was a limit to how long she could postpone the inevitable, she reminded herself grimly. Besides, hiding in her room all day would only let him know how much she had been affected by what had happened last night. The best thing to do was brazen it out as coolly as possible.

With that resolution firmly in mind, she dressed in her usual style—shorts and a T-shirt—and marched herself down to the terrace where breakfast was always served.

Only Dakis was there. He greeted her with a broad grin. '*Yá sas!* You're a sleepy-head this morning—you've just missed Theo.'

'Have I?' she responded in a noncommittal tone, hiding her relief as she took a seat at the table and poured herself a glass of freshly squeezed orange juice.

'He's gone to Ayia Napa,' Dakis announced with satisfaction. 'I have some property over there, and there's a problem come up over letting a couple of shops. I needed someone I could rely on to look into it—couldn't leave it all to that idiot manager.'

'If the manager's an idiot, why did you make him the manager?' Megan enquired mildly.

'Because he does perfectly well so long as I'm around to keep an eye on him. He does what I tell him.'

She smiled, shaking her head. 'Maybe you should try employing people who can cope without you watching their every move?' she suggested. 'Then you wouldn't have to worry all the time.'

'Huh! Where am I going to find people I could trust like that?' he demanded crossly. 'No, it's up to Theo. After all, it'll all be his one day. It's time he started taking a bit of responsibility.'

Megan reached for the pot of honey, and spread a little on her croissant. 'You're not going to disinherit him now that he's engaged to Eleni then?' she enquired, managing to inject a light note of humour into her voice.

'Oh, that!' He snorted in derision. 'I told you, he's not going to marry that silly little *vlaka*. He's just doing it to annoy me.'

Megan didn't respond to that. Instead she glanced around, with every appearance of casual unconcern. 'By the way, where is Eleni this morning?' she enquired. 'She doesn't usually have her breakfast early.'

Dakis grinned in delight. 'Ah, well, that's one good thing that's come out of it. She's persuaded her parents to let Sophia take her to London—to purchase her trousseau. With a bit of luck it'll take them at least a month.'

There was no sign of Theo for the rest of the day, not even at dinner. Megan had to keep a check on her tongue to stop herself asking Dakis whether he had flown straight back to London, to be with his fiancée—the old man was much too shrewd not to notice if she seemed to be taking a particular interest in his son.

With Eleni and Sophia gone, and Giorgos returned to Greece, the villa was unusually quiet. The temperature was soaring into the eighties, so after lunch on the following day, with Dakis settled for his nap, she decided to take a swim in the pool instead of having her usual work-out in the gym.

The water was deliciously cool. In her teens she had been a school champion, and she enjoyed swimming, though she had had little time to do it in recent years. Slicing through the water in a fast crawl, she pushed herself as hard as she could, enjoying the stretching of her muscles, the slight ache of breathlessness as she tumbled at each end of the pool to kick away from the tiled wall and power down another length.

When at last she had exhausted herself, she swam to the edge and pulled a clear plastic Lilo down into the water. She had left her sunglasses and a wide-brimmed straw hat she had bought in Limassol ready beside it, and, hauling herself up onto it, she lay back, relaxing luxuriantly as she bobbed gently on the ripples that lapped across the pool's surface, letting herself drift on the edge of sleep...

'Enjoying your work?'

She opened her eyes, startled, as a sardonic voice cut across her moment of peace. Theo was standing at the poolside, his feet apart, his hands deep in his pockets, looking much too disturbingly handsome in a pair of light cotton chinos and a sleeveless white T-shirt that was stretched taut across the muscles of his wide shoulders.

Since she had spent a particularly difficult morning with Dakis, trying to persuade him to take a little exercise in the gym, she did not appreciate Theo's mocking comment. 'Your father's taking his nap,' she responded tartly.

'I see.'

He was wearing sunglasses, so it was impossible to be sure of how he was looking at her, but she was all too uncomfortably aware of the way her blue swimsuit clung to every contour of her body, intimately defining the firm swell of her breasts, the smooth curve of her stomach. With a nervous gesture she pushed her own sunglasses up her nose, struggling to maintain a façade of cool indifference.

'Was there something you wanted?' she enquired.

His mouth curved into a slow, lazy smile. 'Possibly…' He left the word to hang enigmatically between them, hinting that perhaps he was sufficiently interested in her to want to pursue their last encounter to its logical conclusion—or perhaps he wasn't.

Megan felt her jaw clench with annoyance. For sheer arrogance, he took the gold medal! He clearly believed that she would come running, if and when he should decide to snap his fingers in her direction. Well, he'd find out he was very much mistaken! He had caught her by surprise the other night, that was all—one moment playing the red-hot lover in the gym, the next announcing his engagement to Eleni. She had no intention of allowing herself to play his games again.

It would just be…irritating if he didn't even try, so that she would have no opportunity to put him in his place.

He had strolled over to one of the sun-loungers set out around the pool, and one of the staff had brought out a carafe of orange juice—well chilled, to judge by the mist of frosting on the glass. Stretched out at full length, his arms casually folded behind his head, he was the picture of relaxation—but there was no way that she could relax again.

With a sigh of impatience, she rolled over on the Lilo,

and paddled it back to the edge of the pool, levering herself out onto the side. Unfortunately—inevitably— her towel and T-shirt were on the lounger beside his, so she was forced to walk round the pool towards him.

Though his eyes were still hidden by the sunglasses, she could feel them watching her with every step she took. Somehow she managed to hold herself up with dignity, though with nothing but a clinging skin of blue Lycra to cover her she felt as if she was naked. It was with considerable relief that she was able to reach for her T-shirt, and drag it on over her head—though the mocking curve of his smile told her that he had enjoyed her discomfort.

'Orange juice?' he offered, blandly polite.

'Thank you.' She would have preferred to be able to escape, but there was nowhere she could be sure of being safe from him—not even in her own room. She had little choice but to sit here, sipping her orange juice, struggling to match his sang-froid. 'How did your trip go?' she enquired—at least that should be a safe topic of conversation.

He laughed dryly. 'Pretty well. I shall be able to give Papa a satisfactory report when he wakes up.'

'Good.'

He turned his head to look at her properly. 'How is he?'

She glanced across at him, sensing the seriousness of his concern. 'Making quite good progress,' she responded. 'He's a lot steadier on his feet, and he's getting quite a lot of movement back in his arm. He's still having quite a lot of difficulty with things like shaving and dressing, though—he's still trying to put both arms into the sleeve of his shirt. I suppose it was fortunate that his stroke was on his right side, so it hasn't affected his speech. But his memory and concentration are quite poor—it will be a long job for him to get those back.'

'You think he will?'

'I honestly don't know,' she admitted frankly. 'His stroke was in the medium range of severity, but the recovery he's made so far is encouraging. I think you'll have a clearer picture in a month or so.'

'What if he has another one?'

'It's possible—though just because he's had the one doesn't necessarily mean that he will. And, if he did, it would depend on its severity. It could be much like this one, which would be a set-back but not a disaster...'

'Or?'

'I don't suppose you want me to mince words. A bad one could kill him.'

'I see.' He fell silent, frowning behind his sunglasses.

Megan took a deep breath; it had to be said. 'The less he has to worry about, the better.'

He quirked a questioning eyebrow in her direction. 'Meaning...?'

'Form your own conclusions,' she responded bluntly. 'I don't know much about his business affairs, but I know they're pretty extensive. Unfortunately, you're the only one he'd be willing to trust to take any of it on. If you'd at least take some of the load off him...'

'It would be good for his health?'

'Very good.'

He laughed again, shaking his head. 'If I thought he was really ready to let go of the reins...'

'If you were willing to acknowledge the value of his advice and experience...' she countered bravely.

He returned her a long, level look, as if thinking over what she had said, and then he smiled that slow, lazy, mocking smile that told her he would make his decision in his own good time. 'Maybe.' He stretched his arms above his head, easing the thick knots of muscle in his shoulders. 'I think I'll take a swim. Fancy coming in again?'

'Not just at the moment,' she responded coolly.

'Lazy bones.'

He rose easily to his feet, and in one smooth movement peeled his T-shirt off over his head. Megan struggled not to watch, but she couldn't help herself—her eyes seemed to be drawn towards him of their own volition. His body was lean and hard, the muscles beneath his sun-bronzed skin as defined as a piece of sculpture, and across his wide chest there was a smattering of rough, dark, male hair, arrowing down over the ripple of taut abdominals to disappear below the waistband of his chinos...

She swallowed hard, her hands shaking slightly as she reached for the glass of orange juice on the table beside her. The hint of knowing amusement in his smile warned her that he was perfectly well aware of the fevered images that were swirling in her brain. Mesmerised, she watched as he slowly unfastened the silver buckle on his leather belt, unsnapped the top button of his chinos...

'Sure you won't have that swim?'

'No...' The word came out half-choked, and she had to draw in a sharp breath before she could answer more evenly, 'No, thank you.'

'Pity.'

His hands dropped to the zip of his chinos, sliding it down... For a brief moment she closed her eyes, the tension quivering in her stomach muscles making it difficult to breathe. When she opened them again, he was kicking the chinos aside—but the taut black swimming-trunks moulding his lean hips left little enough to the imagination, and she couldn't prevent the deep flush of colour that swept into her cheeks.

With lithe male grace he paced around to the springboard that was fixed above the deep end of the pool, perfectly balanced as he ran along it and dived, arms outstretched as he soared like a bird and then knifed down into the water, making barely a ripple on its surface.

The moment's respite as he swam with a powerful stroke along the bottom of the pool gave her an opportunity to compose herself. By the time he surfaced at the far end she had picked up her magazine and was leafing idly through it, sparing him no more than a cool glance, her voice laced with sardonic humour as she awarded him points out of ten.

'Nine point seven.'

'Megan! Come and join us!' Dakis waved a wooden mallet in the air as he called to her from the lower lawn, where a croquet pitch had been laid out. 'Between the two of us we can teach this young scoundrel a thing or two, eh?'

Megan had been hoping to slip past unnoticed, but she forced a smile as she turned her footsteps towards the two men. It was almost a month now since Theo and Eleni had announced their engagement. Eleni was still in London, the demands of her trousseau apparently keeping her close to Bond Street and Sloane Square.

The time had seen a considerable improvement in Dakis's condition; some days were better than others, and he was still inclined to get very frustrated by his limitations, but he was mostly able to walk unaided now, except when he was tired, and he was able to concentrate for longer and longer stretches with each day.

The issue with Theo had been less satisfactory. It had been like a game of cat-and-mouse between them, leaving her emotions tangled, her brain in a hopeless jumble of confusion. *Did* he find her attractive? One moment she was half convinced that he did, the next she was just as certain that he was simply mocking her, amusing himself by luring her into betraying by a look or a smile that she was all too vulnerable to the tug of that raw male magnetism, try as she might to maintain her façade of cool indifference.

She hadn't expected him to stay around for so long, nor that he would be able to avoid quarrelling with his father. But he seemed to be making a genuine effort to get along with the old man, and even to encourage him to take the exercise he needed. It was he who had produced this croquet set.

She paused to watch, but shook her head, smiling. 'Croquet? I've never played.'

'Nor have I,' Dakis responded cheerfully. 'That doesn't matter—there aren't too many rules. All you have to do is whack your ball through the hoops, and thump your opponent's ball out of the way if you can. Here—have a mallet.'

She really had no choice but to join in the game as Dakis proceeded to coach her on the finer points as if he were an expert, demonstrating the technique for swinging the mallet and explaining the tactics, generously pointing out where she had gone wrong when her first shot went wide.

'Where did this come from?' she asked Theo as Dakis was lining up to take his turn, studying the lie of the grass like a championship golfer on a match-winning putt.

'It was tucked away in a cupboard somewhere—it hasn't been used since I was a kid.'

'It's ideal,' she approved warmly. 'It gets him walking, and it helps him with judging perspective.'

'Unfortunately it doesn't help his temper a great deal—he's competitive even at this,' Theo murmured with wry amusement as his father thwacked one of his balls out of the way with his own.

'*Thavmasios!* It'll take you at least two shots to line it up and get it through now!' he declared in gleeful triumph.

'The primary objective is to get your own balls through the hoop,' Theo pointed out dryly.

'Hah! If you're scared of a little aggressive play, you should stick to tiddly-winks! My second shot, I think.'

His run of play came to an end with the tricky turn at the top of the lawn, and he moved over to sit down on the low retaining wall that ran around the higher terrace, watching as his son took his shot. It was surely just an unfortunate coincidence that he was caught by a sudden fit of coughing as Theo started his swing.

Theo pulled the shot, a sardonic smile curving that hard mouth. 'Are you all right, Papa? Perhaps you've over-tired yourself?'

'No, no—I'm quite all right,' Dakis insisted. 'Stop talking and take your shot.'

A flicker of amusement lit those blue eyes as Theo lined up his shot again. This time Dakis dropped his mallet at the critical moment, Theo hit the shot a little too hard, and the ball bounced across the grass, out of the field of play.

'Oh, dear—how careless of me! I hope I didn't put you off?' his father queried with a transparent lack of sincerity. 'Never mind—it's only a game. Go on, then, Megan—your turn.'

She lined up carefully, and tapped the ball with her mallet. For a moment it really looked as if it was going to go through the narrow hoop, only a fraction of an inch wider than the ball itself, but at the last moment it veered away and came to rest at the side of the hoop.

'Bad luck!' Dakis cried cheerfully. 'Well, it looks like it's my turn again.'

'Don't dare beat him,' Theo said quietly to her as he came back to her side. 'He's a terribly bad loser.'

It was evident to her as they played that Theo was deliberately letting his father win—not so obviously that he would be aware of it, but subtly turning his strokes to miss the hoop every time he seemed to be getting too far ahead.

'I'm…surprised at you staying here in Cyprus for so long,' she remarked to Theo as they walked around the course, her tone one of studied indifference. 'I'd have thought you'd have gone back to London by now.'

He slanted her a look of dry amusement. 'Did you? Why would you think that?'

She shrugged her slender shoulders in casual unconcern. 'I thought you had business interests there.'

'Nothing that can't get along without me. Besides, I thought you wanted me to play the dutiful son, helping Papa run the Nikolaides empire?'

'I do, but…isn't Eleni still there?'

'Indeed she is,' he responded, an inflection of sardonic humour in his voice. 'All the more reason for me to stay here.'

'If you feel that way already, it doesn't bode too well for a successful marriage,' she commented with a touch of asperity.

He laughed, lazily mocking. 'I appreciate your concern for my future happiness, but I assure you it is misplaced. Eleni and I know exactly what to expect of each other—that seems to me to be an excellent basis for a successful marriage.'

'Some people think love ought to come into it somewhere.'

His eyes conveyed cynical amusement at such a quaint notion. 'That's just so much romantic rubbish,' he returned dryly. 'What people choose to call love is nothing more than pure carnal lust dressed up to look respectable. If people marry for no better reason than that they generally find that it doesn't last the course— and they end up in the divorce courts. Far better to be rational about it in the first place.'

'You don't believe in love?' she queried bleakly.

'Do you?'

'Of course…'

'Were you in love with your fiancé?' he challenged, turning the angle of attack in a direction she hadn't anticipated.

She felt a heated blush colour her cheeks as she floundered for a response. 'Well… I…'

'You were planning to marry him,' he pointed out, ruthlessly pinpointing the flaws in her argument. 'Thus, by your own criterion, you must have been in love with him.'

'I…thought I was,' she admitted weakly. 'I just…realised I'd made a mistake.'

'Exactly. At least you were fortunate enough to recognise it before you'd signed away your life to it. Or, worse, brought along children to add to the misery.'

There was a sudden note of bitterness in his voice, and Megan glanced up at him; his last words had shed an unexpected light on his seemingly cold-hearted attitude. His parents had split up when he'd been only twelve years old—a particularly difficult age. His father, she had heard, had been something of a philanderer. Perhaps if the marriage had been the loveless sort he was proposing to enter into himself his mother might have been more willing to tolerate Dakis's behaviour—but apparently she hadn't.

Given that sort of experience in his childhood, it was perhaps understandable that he should try to ensure that his own marriage didn't go the same way, by contracting what was in effect a marriage of convenience. Though, in spite of his confidence, Megan wasn't sure that Eleni was entirely of the same mind.

'You really think your way will be better?' she countered, her voice echoing her doubt.

He shrugged, untroubled. 'At least it has the virtue of honesty.'

'But not fidelity.'

'True,' he conceded dryly. 'But then, if neither of you is expecting it, neither of you will be hurt by the other's infidelity.'

'You won't mind Eleni taking lovers?' she protested, shocked.

'I'll raise no objection, once she's produced the requisite Nikolaides heir.'

'Well, that sounds fair enough,' she retorted on a note of acid sarcasm. 'What's sauce for the goose is sauce for the gander, I suppose. Or the other way round, in this case.'

'Of course.' He smiled, that slow, lazy, derisive smile that always did strange things to her pulse rate. 'So, you see, there's no reason for you to feel any qualms of conscience.'

She glanced up at him, startled at his remark. 'Why should I feel any qualms of conscience?'

Those blue eyes glinted, wicked as sin. 'About becoming my mistress.'

She drew in a sharp breath, struggling to choke out some kind of response. 'I...am not going to be your mistress!' she protested.

'No?' His voice was low and husky, sensually beguiling.

'No!'

'Come along, you two!' Dakis interrupted them, beaming. 'You're so busy chatting, you're not watching the game. Theo, it's your turn. Hurry up.'

'It's supposed to be a leisurely game, Papa, not a race.' Theo laughed softly as he stepped past Megan to take his shot. 'Do you know you're blushing?' he taunted. 'Why would you do that, if you're so sure?'

She tilted up her chin, meeting those mocking eyes defiantly. He was playing games with her—he had been for weeks. Like the jungle cat she had first likened him to, he had been prowling around her, sometimes showing his teeth, sometimes keeping them hidden, never letting her be sure of her ground. And now, apparently, he had decided the time was ripe to move in for the kill.

His mistress? Just the thought conjured images that swirled in her brain like a fever. For almost a month she had ached with the memory of the way he had kissed her, tormented by the need to feel his strong arms around her. She hadn't been able to look at him without remembering that day by the pool, and the hard, male beauty of his body.

Dammit, how much temptation could one woman stand? His mistress? That was rather a glorified title for what she would be if she succumbed. She would be merely a sexual convenience for the couple of months she remained here. Then she would go back to England, and he would have forgotten all about her in the time it took for her plane to leave the runway—he would have no trouble at all finding someone else to take her place.

But he was right. In spite of her furious denial, she wasn't at all sure that she was going to be able to resist.

Dakis was almost skipping with agitation as Theo lined up for his shot. They were both on the final hoop, and if he succeeded in turning the ball tightly he could be first to the peg. Fortunately Dakis refrained from any further shameless exhibitions of gamesmanship, but it wasn't necessary—Theo's ball just missed the hoop.

Dakis swung his mallet in the air in unabashed delight. He could barely wait for Megan to take her shot before scuttling in. He was in a better position on the hoop than Theo had been, and his ball trickled through with just millimetres to spare on each side.

'That's it! That's it! My extra shot!' he enthused.

It took one more round each, but there was no surprise when Dakis won. Theo slanted Megan a look of dry humour as they both clapped their hands in dutiful congratulation; she couldn't quite suppress a smile of response, though she quickly covered it up by turning to Dakis.

'Well done. That was good fun—we'll have to play again tomorrow.'

'Tomorrow? I'm ready for another game now!'

Theo shook his head. 'Count me out, Papa—I have some calls to make.'

Megan shot him a swift look of gratitude—she had been concerned that Dakis would get over-tired, but experience had taught her that trying to warn him to be sensible was usually counter-productive.

'Huh? Oh, well, all right,' the old man conceded grudgingly. 'But tomorrow I'll thrash you again!'

'I'm sure you will,' Theo responded, laughing. 'Shall we have coffee?'

'Good idea!' Dakis dug into his pocket, and pulled out the handset for the two-way radio system he'd had installed, and, squinting at the buttons, pressed out the code for the kitchen. *'Anna? Trees kafes, steen taratsa. Parakalo,'* he barked—though the 'please' at least was an improvement for which Megan felt she could take some credit.

He led the way up to the terrace—Megan noted that he did seem a little tired, but he had been on his feet for over an hour, which was the longest he had managed so far. It was good to see him making such a good recovery—and she was honest enough to admit that Theo had made the greatest contribution towards it.

Not only had he been willing to accede to the old man's frequent demands that he should run hither and thither all over the island on visits to one part of the business or another, but he had apparently been content to spend his evenings losing game after game of draughts or backgammon.

The maid had brought the coffee, and a plate of Dakis's favourite honey-drenched *kataifi* pastries, when he leaned back in his seat, easing his weakened arm. 'I've been thinking,' he announced. 'I really ought to take a little trip over to Kouklia and Ayia Marinouda this week.'

Theo raised his eyes heavenwards; this was his father's usual preamble to sending him off on another errand. 'Why, Papa?' he enquired with admirable restraint.

'To see how the vines are doing, of course. It's very important at this time of year.'

'Don't you think your farm managers are capable of caring for the vines properly?' Theo countered in dry tones.

'There's no harm in checking on them,' Dakis insisted. 'It keeps them on their toes.'

Theo sighed. 'Very well, Papa—if you think it necessary to bother them, I'll go,' he offered.

'Are you sure?' Did the old man really believe anyone was fooled by that paper-thin façade of innocence? 'I wouldn't want to put you to any inconvenience. If you've something else planned...'

'I don't have anything planned, Papa. I'll go tomorrow.'

'Excellent!' A devious glint appeared in those sharp old eyes. 'Why don't you take Megan with you?' he suggested blandly. 'It would give her a chance to see some of the most beautiful parts of the island.'

She shook her head quickly, aghast at the suggestion. 'Oh, no! I...couldn't possibly!' she protested. 'I couldn't leave you on your own.'

'I won't be alone,' he pointed out in a tone of sweet reason. 'I've got a whole houseful of servants here, sitting around with nothing to do. I'll be perfectly all right without you. You haven't had a single day off since you arrived—I don't want people accusing me of being a slave-driver. Off you go, and do a little sightseeing. Don't you worry about me.'

Theo was watching her, his eyes conveying a challenge. 'I don't think she wants to come with me,' he put in, softly provocative.

'Why ever not?' Dakis demanded. 'Surely you're not afraid that people might gossip? Don't you worry about that—it's only an innocent little drive around the island.

What could be wrong with that? You go and have a nice time, and don't give it another thought.'

Theo quirked one sardonic eyebrow in her direction, waiting for her response. To her chagrin, she could think of no reasonable excuse. And if she simply refused to go with him it would be a tacit acknowledgement that she was afraid of him—or, more accurately, afraid that she couldn't keep her own wayward desires under control.

'Well, if you're sure you'll be all right, Dakis,' she conceded reluctantly.

'Of course I will,' he assured her, his satisfaction transparent. 'I'll be fine.'

From beneath her lashes, she slanted him a look of wry suspicion. What was he up to, the old reprobate, throwing her at Theo like this? Did he think it would be enough to persuade Theo not to marry Eleni after all? If so, it wouldn't work. It would suit Theo very well to make her his mistress, but he would still go ahead with his marriage.

CHAPTER SEVEN

MEGAN was glad she had taken the precaution of wearing a sun-hat, as well as smothering herself with a generous amount of high-factor sun-cream. They had set off quite early, but already the sun was hot, blazing down from a cloudless blue sky, its glare bouncing mercilessly from the white chalky cliffs on each side of the road.

Out of half a dozen cars Theo could have selected from his father's garage, he had chosen an open-topped Land Rover, and its powerful V8 engine was making very light work of the kilometres on the wide dual carriageway.

She had made up her mind to take this day exactly as it had been suggested to her—as an opportunity to see a little of the island. She certainly wasn't going to let Theo know how aware she was of him—though when she had first seen him this morning, in a pair of stone-coloured linen trousers and a crisp white short-sleeved shirt, open at the collar to show just a glimpse of the dark cluster of hair at the base of his throat, her heart had started to beat an uncomfortable tattoo against her ribs.

'We'll stop off here first,' Theo announced, flicking the indicator, and turned down a slip-road towards the old road into Limassol. 'The new hotel is due to open next week, and Papa wants me to check that everything's ready. It shouldn't take too long.'

'Fine,' she responded evenly.

But her air of cool unconcern was somewhat dented

when she saw the hotel. Huge and white like an ocean liner, every balcony was decked with flowers, and the flags of a dozen nations waved jauntily from the flag-poles ranged along the front of the lush gardens which separated it from the road.

Theo drew the Land Rover to a halt by the wide mar-ble steps that led up to the smoked-glass entrance doors. It seemed that they were expected—a smart commis-sionaire, immaculate in yellow and turquoise-blue livery, stepped up to welcome them with a salute, and the doors slid open to reveal a deputation of men in grey business suits and crisp white shirts lined up waiting for them.

Theo swung himself out of the Land Rover, the casual ease of his manner in no way undermining the subtle air of authority he conveyed. Megan hesitated, not sure whether to follow him, but he paused as he climbed the steps, clearly expecting that she would. 'Come on,' he urged, his smile lightly teasing. 'You can give me the woman's point of view on the place.'

She didn't return the smile as she clambered out of the Land Rover. It hadn't occurred to her before, but suddenly the potential awkwardness of the situation struck her forcibly. The staff of the hotel would surely know of his engagement to Eleni, and were bound to speculate about the identity of the mysterious woman accompanying him on his tour of inspection.

But then if he wasn't bothered about it why should she care? she reflected tartly. In a couple of months she would be returning home to England, leaving the gossip behind. The only one to be hurt would be Eleni—and perhaps it would do her a favour if she was forced to see what her life would be like if she went ahead with this travesty of a marriage.

She managed some kind of bland response as she was

introduced with some formality to the welcome committee, and then they were ushered into the reception area, where the hotel's general manager proceeded to point out with some pride the key features, explaining the kind of service that guests would receive.

It had certainly earned the five stars it proudly displayed on a plaque above the long cedar-wood reception desk, Megan mused, looking around with interest. No expense had been spared on the sumptuous decor. Acres of sparkling white marble and blue-tinted glass seemed to trap the sun, and the restful sound of trickling water came from a stunning artificial waterfall that cascaded down over a high tower of Perspex cubes reaching to the level of the third floor.

Theo slanted her a questioning look. 'What do you think?'

Her eyes glinted humorously as she affected a non-committal shrug. 'Not bad,' she drawled with exaggerated nonchalance. 'I'd have to see the rest of it before I made up my mind.'

The general manager looked a little hurt, not understanding the joke, but Theo grinned appreciatively. 'Oh, I think you'll find it's pretty much up to the same standard,' he assured her. 'Shall we take a look at the dining room?'

Megan couldn't deny that she was absolutely fascinated by the tour. They visited not only the front of house, where the six hundred guests would be able to enjoy the most pampered luxury, but also the behind-the-scenes kitchens and offices, the laundry room and storerooms, and even the vast underground complex where the heating and air-conditioning plants hummed with economic efficiency.

Finally they returned to Reception, where the whole

staff, smartly turned out in uniforms of sunshine-yellow and turquoise-blue, in varying styles according to the department they worked in, were lined up like a small army on parade. And, like a general inspecting his troops, Theo walked along the ranks, exchanging a few words here and there, nodding with approval at a particularly immaculate turn-out.

Watching him as he stood before the serried rows, addressing a few words to all of them—a pre-opening pep-talk, Megan guessed, though her Greek was nowhere near good enough yet to understand what he was saying—she was forced to recognise the vast gulf that separated them. It wasn't just the money issue— Oh, that shouldn't matter, but she would be a fool to deny that it did.

No, it was much more than that. She was seeing him now as he was, virtually master of all he surveyed— while she would have put herself in maybe the second or third rank of those now listening to him with such respectful attention. Employee, mistress…there was little difference between the two. Except that the former wasn't required to sacrifice her self-respect.

They had spent a few hours at the hotel, and it was late morning before they set off again. The sun was quite fierce now, and Megan crammed her sun-hat tighter onto her head as they turned back onto the dual carriageway to circle around the landward side of the town and on west along the coast.

'So what did you really think of the place?' Theo queried, slanting her a smile that told her he already knew the answer.

'Fabulous!' she admitted with a wry laugh. 'I bet it costs a king's ransom to stay there.'

'It's a five-star hotel, with five-star prices. A lot of

the clientele are likely to be Russian—the new rich businessmen, looking to spend their roubles on a little western decadence. And Papa knows exactly how to help them do just that!'

'He owns several hotels, doesn't he?' Megan asked.

'Four here in Cyprus, and several more in Greece, as well as one in Malta, and an interest in a couple in Egypt. Then there's the holiday apartments—I forget exactly how many. And of course the two cruise-ships. Plus shopping malls, car rentals, vineyards, olives…'

Megan gave him a crooked smile. 'I didn't realise he owned as much as that! I suppose it's not really surprising that the family are all so paranoid that some little gold-digger will come along and try to get her sticky fingers on a slice of it.'

'That's very understanding of you,' he commented dryly. 'I'm surprised you took the job, with us all being so obnoxious to you. A few months in the sun hardly seems an adequate recompense.'

A slight blush of pink coloured her cheeks; he was a little too close to the truth for comfort. She shrugged her slender shoulders in what she hoped was a casual gesture. 'It didn't really matter—*I* knew you were wrong, and so did Dakis. Besides, he needed a nurse, and I was afraid that anyone he hired from an agency wouldn't last a week.'

Those blue eyes flickered with amusement. 'I must admit, I've never known anyone handle him as well as you do.'

'Practice,' she responded lightly. 'And I like him.'

He looked decidedly startled at that. 'You do? You must be one of very few.'

She laughed. 'Oh, I know he can be a bad-tempered old so-and-so at times, but he has the capacity to laugh at himself—and that's quite rare. And after some of the consultants I've had to deal with he's a pussy-cat.'

He laughed too. 'You enjoy nursing?' he asked in a conversational tone.

'I love it! It's not the sort of job you can do if your heart's only half in it.'

'So you're planning to pick up your career again when you go back to England?'

'Of course. Though I'm not really quite sure in what field,' she mused aloud. 'When I first went to work for the agency, it was just a kind of stop-gap, until I found a post like my old one—theatre sister. But now... I'm not so sure. The problem in Theatre is that you don't really get a chance to know the patients—they're mostly unconscious! And, having gone back to "people" nursing, I've realised how much I missed it. I suppose it seems a shame to waste all that training, but maybe I could do some teaching, and combine it with something else. Community nursing, perhaps?'

He arched one dark eyebrow quizzically. 'Bathing old ladies and bandaging their legs?'

'That isn't all there is to it,' she retorted, smiling. 'Anyway, I don't have to make my mind up just yet— there's still two months left of my contract with your father. And I'm in no hurry to go back to England,' she added, leaning back luxuriantly in her seat and tipping up her face to the sun. 'I bet it's raining.'

'Eleven degrees Celsius, and showers, according to Eleni,' he reported.

Ah, yes—Eleni. Foolishly, she had almost let herself forget about his fiancée. In fact, chatting to him so easily like this, she had almost begun to let herself like him. Which could be very dangerous, she warned herself sharply. He had made his intentions perfectly clear.

They had left the busy outskirts of Limassol behind, and, after passing through the British Army base of Akrotiri, the road began to wind its way along the coast, sometimes forging inland between the sun-baked chalk cliffs dotted with scrubby thorn bushes, sometimes offering spectacular glimpses of the sparkling Mediterranean.

They had driven for a little over half an hour when Theo pulled the car off onto a lay-by at the side of the road, right on the edge of the cliffs. 'Sightseeing,' he remarked with a flicker of sardonic amusement. 'We're in luck—there's usually a squadron of tourist coaches here.'

There was just one other car, and an ice-cream van. Intrigued, Megan scrambled out of the car, and followed Theo over to the vantage point at the top of the cliff. Below her, the sea had scooped out a shallow bay with a pebble beach, punctuated by a tumble of white rocks that seemed to have been tossed out into the shimmering sapphire water by a giant's careless hand.

'This is where love was born,' Theo murmured, his voice taking on a husky timbre.

Megan felt her heart kick sharply against her ribs, and she stared up at him, her startled eyes betraying too much of what she had been trying so hard to keep secret.

'Aphrodite, the goddess of love,' he teased mockingly. 'Born from the foam of the sea.'

'Oh…' She swallowed hard, drawing in a sharp breath as she struggled to hold onto her fragile equilibrium. 'It's…a lovely place. Wait—I must take a picture.'

Quickly she turned back to the car, and picked up her camera from the back seat. Fiddling with it, checking that the film was wound on to the right place, gave her a few precious moments to restore her composure. He was playing games with her again, hinting at things that stirred dangerous ideas in her fevered brain, and then drawing back, mocking her for reacting. She was going to have to try to keep a stricter control of her imagination, or by the end of the day she would be ready for the mad-house!

Theo was standing close to the low barrier at the edge of the cliff, that familiar smile curving his mouth, those incredible blue eyes seeming to reflect the colour of the sea behind him. She lifted the camera, centring him in the frame. 'Say cheese!'

He laughed lazily as she took the snap. 'I ought to take one of you.'

The couple from the other car turned from admiring the view. 'I'll take one of both of you, if you'll take one of us with our camera,' the man offered.

'Oh... No, it's all right,' Megan protested quickly. 'I mean...I'll take one of you, if you like, but...'

'Don't be silly, Megan,' Theo drawled with indolent humour. 'Come and have your picture taken.'

He held out his hand to her, and she felt an odd little constriction in her throat as she walked over to him. He slipped his arm around her shoulders as if it was the most natural thing in the world, drawing her to his side. She glanced up at him a little uncertainly as the man clicked the camera.

'There! I'll just take another one—for luck. Smile!'

Somehow she managed some kind of rigid grin, relieved when she was able to escape from Theo's side. She watched as he took the other man's camera, nodding patiently at his fussy explanation of how to use it and waiting while the couple posed themselves exactly right against the spectacular backdrop.

Her own camera she cradled carefully in her hands.

She didn't want to risk damaging it, not until she had a chance to take this film out, with its precious image of Theo. At least she would have that to hold onto, to keep vivid the memories if time should start to fade them. Though she doubted that it ever would.

The photographs taken, they were back on the road within a few minutes. Their next stop was at a vineyard a couple of miles further on, a short distance up a narrow track that led from the main road. The manager, it turned out, was the son of one of Dakis's legion of cousins, and he and his family welcomed Theo with a mixture of affection and deference, urging them into the plain cottage where a well-scrubbed pine table was almost tottering under the weight of the lunch that awaited them.

They seemed to accept Megan's presence without any trace of curiosity or surprise—theirs not to question the hand that fed them, she supposed. Most of them spoke at least a little English, except for the elderly grandmother and the youngest of the five children, but much of the conversation was necessarily in Greek—from what she could pick up, it was mostly about the prospects of good weather for the growing season, and exactly when would be the right moment to harvest.

After a long, leisurely meal, they strolled through the rows of vines, interspersed with plantings of cherry and peach trees, as Theo discussed with the vineyard manager the niceties of pruning—how to select which shoots to retain and which to rub off, the advantages of cluster-thinning to ensure an improved quality of grape and preserve the vigour of the vine. Megan listened, intrigued and a little surprised that he knew so much about viticulture.

'Ah, it's in the blood of every Cypriot,' he responded, laughing, when she commented on it. 'The wines of

Cyprus were famous even in the days of King Solomon, and Mark Antony gave the island to Cleopatra because she loved the sweetness of our wine. And legend has it that Sultan Selim II ordered the invasion of Cyprus after tasting the wine—perhaps making it something of a liability. Anyway, we've just about finished here now—let's get going.'

The visit to the second vineyard was much briefer, but by the time they left it was late afternoon. Megan had automatically assumed that they would turn back towards Limassol, but instead Theo turned right again as they reached the main road, towards Paphos.

'Where are we going now?' she asked, curious.

He slanted her an enigmatic smile. 'You've seen the place where Aphrodite was born—I thought you might like to see the place where she's supposed to have bathed.'

'Oh…yes,' she agreed, reluctant to admit even to herself that she was in no hurry for this day to end. 'That sounds…nice. Is it far?'

'Not all that far. There's a restaurant just outside Polis owned by some more of my father's cousins—we can have dinner there. A traditional Cypriot dinner—*meze*.'

'What's that?'

'You'll see. I hope you're hungry?'

She nodded, laughing. 'I'm always hungry! It must be all the fresh sea air. If I'm not careful, I shall look like a barrel by the time I go home.'

'Oh, I don't think there's much danger of that,' he remarked, letting his eyes slide lazily over her slim figure. 'You look in excellent shape to me.'

She felt a hot blush of pink rise to her cheeks, and turned her head away quickly, focusing all her attention on the passing countryside.

The outskirts of Paphos were much like Limassol—
lots of low, square houses with what she took to be wa-
ter-tanks on the roof, and dusty industrial areas enclosed
by wire fencing. But they didn't go far into town before
they turned off again, heading north on a road signposted
for Polis.

This western side of the island was much greener than
the southern coast, and the air was fragrant with the
scent of orange and lemon trees in full bloom. Here and
there were olive groves, some of the twisted trunks a
yard thick, the silvery leaves rustling softly in the breeze.

At first the road climbed up into the hills, passing
crumbling white villages clustered around square-
towered churches, though fewer and fewer of them appeared as they climbed higher. Their companions on the
road were mostly dusty lorries throwing out fumes of
diesel, or noisy mopeds buzzing like demented hornets,
or the occasional sleek Mercedes. But the older form of
transport—the plodding donkey, with its load of wicker
panniers—had not been completely superseded. And at
one particularly awkward bend in the road they came
across a flock of goats, being shepherded by a boy of
about twelve who was proudly sporting a Los Angeles
Dodgers baseball cap.

As they reached the highest ridge of the hills, the landscape opened out in front of them in tumbling valleys
of thorny scrub and neatly tended vineyards. Far away
to the right they could see the higher peaks of the
Troödos mountains, misty on the horizon, as the road
wound its way down a long, fertile valley towards the
north-west coast of the island.

The afternoon was fading into a hazy blue dusk as
they drove through the picturesque little town of Polis,
and turned west again onto a road that ran right along

the edge of the sea. There was hardly a breeze, and the water was almost still, lapping against the shingle beach like the softest whisper. Wild flowers grew all along the edge of the road—tiny purple gentians, yellow primroses, and swathes of pretty white bell-flowers.

A few miles beyond the town they came to a small fishing village, its narrow streets a challenge to the convoy of tourist coaches that were heading the other way. Theo had to pull the Land Rover onto the pavement to let them pass.

'That's right—all go home,' he murmured, smiling in sardonic humour at the sunburned, sweaty faces inside the coaches. 'Leave Akámas to its peaceful sleep.'

'You don't seem to like tourists very much, considering your father makes so much of his money out of them,' Megan remarked dryly.

He conceded a wry laugh. 'You're calling me a hypocrite? Well, yes, I suppose you're right, to some extent. But it's a dilemma that's very difficult to resolve. Cyprus has always welcomed travellers—even though in previous centuries they usually came in the guise of invaders. And there's no doubt that the tourist industry is vital to the economy. But the price is high when the sheer weight of numbers begins to destroy the very fabric of what they have come to see.

'Take this place—the Akámas peninsula.' He waved his hand to indicate the wild, empty landscape to the west of the road. 'Up to now, it's remained unspoilt—but for how long? Some of the best beaches in Cyprus are along this coast, but so are the breeding grounds of some of the most endangered turtles of the Mediterranean. Last year I persuaded my father to buy up some of the land, to protect it for conservation, but trying to get others to do the same is a very slow process.'

Megan slanted him a look of some surprise. She had thought of him as totally selfish, interested only in his own entertainment, but these past few weeks she had been obliged to revise her opinion of him. First there had been his genuine concern for his father, and now this evidence of his interest in so unlikely a subject as endangered turtles.

But he was still the same man who had so little regard for women that he had tried to make love to one on the very night he had become engaged to another, she reminded herself forcefully. The same man who had made it quite clear that he wanted her to be his mistress.

Perhaps she should have insisted that they return to the villa on leaving the second vineyard, she mused a little uneasily. Soon it would be night, and they were a long way from home. She would never have agreed to this excursion to visit Aphrodite's Pool if she had realised how far it was... Would she?

The village petered out into a row of open-air tavernas right on the edge of the beach. Theo drew the car into the kerb outside one of them, and tooted the horn. A young waiter in a crisp white shirt and black silk bow-tie, taking an order from one of the tables, glanced up, a look of surprise and delight spreading across his face, and, abandoning his customers, he came out to greet Theo, his arms spread wide to embrace him.

'*Éla, Maláka! Ti néa?*'

Theo laughed, responding in kind. From the kitchen at the back of the restaurant several enquiring faces appeared, and as Theo was recognised a cry of delight went up. In moments the entire family were out—small children up to grandparents and great-grandparents—slapping Theo on the back and hugging him, chattering in rapid Greek.

Megan climbed out of the Land Rover, again hovering uncertainly in the background until Theo managed to detach himself from the throng, and drew her forward.

'This is Nurse Taylor.' He introduced her with a formality she felt as some relief. 'She's come over from England to care for Papa while he's ill. But today is her day off, so I'm taking her sightseeing.'

The young waiter bowed over her hand with exaggerated gallantry. 'Welcome to Cyprus, *kiria orea*,' he greeted her. 'I hope you are enjoying your visit?'

'Very much,' she responded warmly. 'It's a beautiful island.'

'And of course you have the best tour guide in my good cousin,' he assured her, mock-solemn. 'Though he deigns to visit us but rarely. But come—you will stay to dinner?'

'Of course,' Theo asserted, laughing. 'That's why we came.'

'Splendid!'

It seemed that the customers were entirely forgotten as, with the greatest possible fuss and commotion, three or four tables were shifted together. Tablecloths were spread, plates and glasses set out, baskets of fresh sesame bread brought from the kitchen. Megan was ushered to a seat beside Theo as the whole family gathered around the table, and several bottles of wine were uncorked, even the smallest child raising a glass liberally diluted with mineral water.

'Yá sas!'

Megan responded to the toast with a shy smile, a little overwhelmed by the noisy enthusiasm of the party. Even some of the people from the neighbouring restaurants had strolled along to see what was happening, drawing up extra chairs around the table as plate after plate of food was carried out from the kitchen.

'This is *meze*?' she whispered to Theo, amazed at the variety—and the quantity—spread out before her.

He nodded. 'You have to pace yourself,' he warned, a lilt of amusement in his voice. 'It takes stamina to do justice to a full table of *mezedes*.'

Megan could well believe the truth of that. There were bowls of salad, moist with tomatoes and aubergines and piquant with garlic, dishes of pickled capers and spicy squid, plates of smoked sausages and marinated ham, and grilled halloumi cheese, as well as half a dozen types of dip. And just when she thought the table would collapse under the weight of it all the pièce de résistance appeared—three charcoal grills, piled with sizzling kebabs of lamb and beef.

It seemed that the polite thing to do was to help yourself, using your fingers or a hunk of bread, and she soon got the hang of it, dipping into every dish in a spirit of experimentation, greedily coming back for more of her favourites.

The sun was setting, bathing the tranquil sea with a coppery glow and taking the sting out of the heat of the day. As the sky turned from cobalt-blue to black, and the stars began to come out, a couple of the men brought out musical instruments—a bouzouki and a guitar—and began to sing some of the haunting Cypriot folk songs.

The soft whisper of the sea was like a counterpoint to the sweet melodies, and Megan drew in a long, deep breath, letting it go on a soundless sigh as she slanted a covert glance up at the man at her side. It was such a romantic evening, so full of the poignant whisper of 'if only'...

As the evening wore on, the table became littered with the debris of the meal, though there were still a few titbits to nibble at. No one seemed to be in a hurry to bring the party to an end. Some of the men had cleared a larger space between the tables, and now they were dancing the classical slow, pacing line-dance of Greece, their arms laced over each other's shoulders, each step placed with a careful deliberation.

Theo's cousin—the one who had first welcomed him—called out to him to join in, and with a good-natured laugh he went, slipping into the line as the others cheered and lacing his arms over his cousins' shoulders, following the steps with familiar ease even when the syncopated rhythm speeded up, faster and faster, as the women clapped along.

At last most of the dancers gave up and left the floor, leaving it to just two die-hards who were performing what looked like a kind of belly-dance to the mournful notes of the bouzouki. The moon had risen—it had passed through its ancient cycle, and now it was full again, the way it had been that night when Theo had announced his engagement to Eleni... But she didn't want to remember Eleni tonight. For a little while, she wanted to forget that the damned girl even existed.

Theo had returned to his seat beside her; with the crush around the table he was very close, his hand resting loosely over the back of her chair, just brushing against the nape of her neck—a casual enough gesture, one that could easily have been accidental. But she didn't think it was.

Maybe she should have been a little more sparing with the wine, she reminded herself a little belatedly. But it was such an exceptional wine—she had never tasted anything quite like it. Liquid ruby in the glass, it had a

silky elegance on the tongue, sweet and rich and star-
tlingly heady—she could feel its warmth coursing
through her veins, heightening the sense that she was in
some kind of dream.

She had no idea how late it was by the time the party
finally began to break up. Most of the children had fallen
asleep on laps, and were carefully carried away to bed
as Theo's cousin Costas walked with them back to the
Land Rover.

'You are staying now in Cyprus?' he asked Theo.

Theo paused, considering his response. 'It isn't decided yet. A lot depends on how well Papa recovers from
his stroke.'

'Of course.' Costas nodded solemnly. 'God grant him
good health. But you will be back to see us, yes? Do
not leave it so long this time.'

Theo grinned, slapping his cousin's back. 'I'll be
back. *Yá sas!*'

'*Yá sas,*' Costas responded. He turned to Megan, and
again took her hand, this time raising it to his lips, his
liquid brown eyes gazing deeply into hers. 'And you,
kiria orea,' he murmured huskily. 'You too will come
back to visit us, yes?'

She laughed a little unsteadily. 'Maybe... Before I go
back to England.'

He kissed her fingertips again, squeezing her hand and
only letting it go with some reluctance as she climbed
into the Land Rover. And then, with more cries of '*Yá
sas!*', they drove off, waving to the crowd left behind in
the restaurant.

Megan yawned as she sat back in her seat. 'That was
good.'

Theo gave her an enigmatic smile. 'I'm glad you enjoyed it.'

The thought passed fleetingly through her mind that she should definitely not have drunk so much wine; she usually drank very little, and it seemed to have gone straight to her head. 'What did that word mean?' she asked, struggling to make some kind of casual conversation. 'The one that your cousin kept using—*"kiria orea"*?'

Theo laughed softly. 'It means "beautiful lady". He was trying to flirt with you.'

'Oh…!' She laughed a little uncertainly. 'How silly.'

'Very silly,' he agreed. 'You're already spoken for.'

His voice conveyed a quiet certainty, and Megan found herself unable to argue with him. It had been inevitable, from the moment she had agreed to come on this excursion—from the moment she had agreed to come to Cyprus. Somehow she seemed to be losing her grip on all the rational, common-sense arguments that should have been her defence, and in their place there was only…temptation…

'I…thought we were going to visit Aphrodite's Pool,' she managed, her voice alarmingly unsteady.

'We are. The only time to visit is by moonlight.'

'But…won't it be closed?' she protested.

'Not for us.'

No, it wouldn't be, she reflected wryly. That was why he gave the impression of being a man who always got what he wanted—quite simply, he always did.

'Is it…far?'

'We're there.'

CHAPTER EIGHT

A TORCH flashed out at them from beneath the shadow of a tree, and a voice called softly to Theo, *'Endaksi, Kirios Nikolaides?'*

Megan had picked up enough Greek to realise that they were expected, and that the security guard was checking that everything was okay. 'Do you...make a habit of this kind of nocturnal sightseeing trip?' she queried dryly.

He returned her a faintly mocking smile. 'Not exactly a habit, no,' he responded, acknowledging the guard's greeting with a brief wave of his hand. Swinging the car in a sharp turn to the right, he parked it where the road ended.

For a moment the only sound was the quiet ticking of the engine as it cooled, and then a silence, deeper than anything Megan had ever heard, washed around them. By day, she would guess, this was probably quite a busy tourist attraction, but now the car park was empty and the little shop in darkness, leaving the place to slip back into the realms of moonlight.

Somewhere in the distance an owl hooted. Megan drew in a long, slow breath; it was almost as if they had strayed into a dream. The twentieth century seemed unreal—they were in a mythical time, before the dawn of history, when gods and goddesses had walked the earth.

The night air had sobered her up somewhat, and the light-headedness she felt now had little to do with the wine she had drunk. Her heart was fluttering in a kind of tense anticipation; that small, niggling voice in her head was warning her that it probably wasn't a very sensible idea to be here. But she had spent twenty-nine years being sensible—tonight the moon and Aphrodite were weaving their spells, and she was a captive of her own heart.

Theo took her hand, and led her up a narrow path through the trees that was barely wide enough for one person, the moon giving them just enough light to pick their way. 'Careful,' he warned as they came to a few shallow flagstone steps. A heavy branch hung over the path, and she ducked beneath it. 'We're almost there.'

Just ahead, down a few more shallow steps, was a small clearing. The moonlight filtering down through the leaves above her showed Megan that she was at the bottom of a deep, rocky glade, the steep walls thickly overgrown with ferns and shrubs. The air was filled with the scent of damp earth and the sound of trickling water. Looking around, her eyes now grown more accustomed to the darkness, she saw to her left a deep overhang of rock, enclosing a small natural pool. In the moonlight the water had a misty glow, like breath on a mirror.

'Aphrodite's Pool,' Theo murmured, his voice huskily sensual. 'This is where she would come to bathe, naked, and to tryst in secret with her lovers. The legends say that if you look into the pool at midnight, when the moon is full—just as it was when Aphrodite bathed— you will see the face of your own lover.'

Megan laughed a little unsteadily at the romantic myth, but in spite of her scepticism some strange power was drawing her towards the pool.

'What do you see?' he challenged softly, so close behind her that his warm breath stirred her hair.

Shadows, the shimmering reflection of the moon...

She leaned over further, and saw her own face, her hair
like a pale halo around her head. And beside her, tall
and dark like some ancient Greek god come down again
from distant Mount Olympus, was Theo. The face of her
lover…

'Well…?'

She turned slowly from the pool, lifting her eyes to
meet his, letting herself drown in their hypnotic blue
depths. Her heartbeat was a fevered flutter, her mouth
dry; some kind of magic was shimmering between them,
as ancient as the rocks, as insubstantial as moonlight.

Slowly he lifted his hand and brushed it along her
cheek. 'I want you,' he murmured. 'Every beautiful inch
of you.' He bent his head, his mouth brushing over hers,
taunting, tantalising, making her ache for more. 'Take
your clothes off.' His voice was gruff, commanding her
will. 'I want to see you as naked as Aphrodite.'

She caught her breath, slightly shocked, but it was as
if she was held in his power, unable to resist him. Taking
a step back from him, she put her hands to the top button
of her sun-dress, unfastening it slowly—and then the
next, and the next, so that the fabric fell loosely aside,
offering him a subtle glimpse of the shadowed valley
between her breasts.

'All of them,' he insisted. He had leaned back against
a spur of rock, watching her, his hands thrust deep into
the pockets of his chinos, languidly relaxed. But she saw
his throat move with the tension, and with a sudden frisson of excitement she recognised that he was not as
coolly controlled as he was pretending to be.

Something seemed to spark inside her—something of
the spirit of the ancient goddess of love herself. Holding
his eyes with hers, she let her hands drop to the lowest
button of her dress, a little above her knee, and slowly,

letting her hands linger tantalisingly at each one, she unfastened them all the way up, until there was just a single one at her waist holding the dress together.

Her eyes glinted with Aphrodite's spell as she slid that last button very slowly through the buttonhole, and with one graceful movement shrugged the dress back over the curve of her shoulders, casting it aside. The dainty white lace of her bra and briefs glimmered in the moonlight, gossamer against the sun-kissed bronze of her skin.

He let his gaze slide down over her in a lingering appraisal, but still he didn't move. 'I said naked,' he reminded her, a rasp of gravel in his throat.

She drew in a long, slow breath; she knew all the rational reasons why she shouldn't be doing this, but rational thought had no place in what was happening now—if it had, she wouldn't even be here. A smile of wanton wickedness curved her soft mouth as her hands moved to the clasp that nestled between the firm swell of her breasts. He was breathing a little more heavily as he watched her, but as she unfastened the clasp his breathing seemed to stop.

The moonlight shimmered silver on her skin, highlighting the creamy contours of her breasts, pertly tipped with buds of rosy pink. A hot little glow of anticipation ignited inside her as she remembered the last time he had looked at her like this, the way he had caressed her. That night he had walked away, but he wouldn't be walking away tonight.

His blue eyes glinted with undisguised appreciation as she moved with graceful elegance, turning slightly, lifting her arms above her head to treat him to a glimpse of every angle. She was enjoying herself, behaving in ways she would never have dreamed of, inspired by the mythical patroness of sexual desire.

He still hadn't moved, but she could sense the powerful tension of male arousal in him. He had said he wanted her to be his mistress. There was no promise in that of how long he would want her, of anything beyond the simple gratification of a purely physical appetite. But she didn't care; she wanted to surrender to every demand he made of her, to feel the hard strength of that male body pinning her down, crushing her beneath his weight, thrusting into her with his fierce possession.

'Naked.' She whispered the promise as her hands slid slowly down over her body to the tiny lace scrap of her briefs, the final veil. They slithered down over her slender thighs, pooling around her ankles, and she stepped out of them, casting them aside with her other clothing.

An odd little flutter of tension was coiling in the pit of her stomach as she turned to face him, offering every inch of her naked body for his pleasure. She could feel the heat of his gaze as it lingered for what seemed like an eternity over the firm, ripe swell of her breasts, the peach-smooth curve of her stomach, dimpled by her dainty navel, and on…to the soft crown of honey-brown curls at the crest of her thighs.

'Well?' She stretched her arms high above her head, conscious of the way the movement invitingly lifted her breasts, and turned a slow pirouette before him. 'Is this what you want?' The warning glint in his eyes told her that indeed it was, but as he made a move towards her she skipped up onto the low rocks that surrounded Aphrodite's Pool. 'You'll have to come and get me, then,' she taunted, mischievous as a sprite, luring him on with her provocative retreat as she splashed into the pool.

The water was as cool and fresh as champagne, and she laughed, stooping to scoop up handfuls of it to splash

at him. It scattered over him in sparkling drops—she
wouldn't have been surprised to see it turn to steam as
it touched him. He stepped across the low barrier of
rocks, not deterred by the water, the glitter of amusement
in his eyes detracting not one degree from the relentless
intent she could sense in him as he pursued her into the
shadowy recesses of the pool.

A slippery rock beneath her foot almost threw her off
balance, and his hand reached out to steady her, clamp-
ing around her arm like a steel manacle. Her playful
defiance evaporated with a small gasp of shock as she
stared up at him, recognising from the hard set of his
jaw that the time for teasing was over; this was serious.

Without a word he dragged her roughly into his arms,
almost crushing her, as his mouth came down to claim
hers with a savage intensity that would brook no resistance. But resistance was the last thing on her mind. Her
lips parted in sweet invitation, welcoming the plundering
invasion of his tongue deep into the lush, moist corners
of her mouth as her spine arched to curve her supple
body even closer to his, thrilled by the delicious abrasion
of his clothing against her soft, naked skin.

The heat between them was igniting a conflagration,
threatening to consume them both. His breathing was
ragged, his hands rough with urgency as they caressed
her, but her own hunger was as fierce as his, fuelled by
the uncertainty of the past few weeks, of not knowing
if he really wanted her or not.

Impatient for the touch of his naked flesh against hers,
she tugged at his shirt, dragging it off over his head and
tossing it over to where her own clothes lay in a jumbled
heap. Then she wrapped her arms around his waist and
pressed herself against the hard wall of his chest, the

smattering of coarse male body-hair across his warm skin tickling her cheek.

His hand tangled in her hair, dragging her head back, and his mouth came down on hers again, hot and greedy, taking all she offered and demanding more. Even the chill of the water couldn't cool their blood as they tumbled and splashed in it; she hadn't been aware that Theo had slipped out of his chinos, but now she felt the brush of his bare thigh against hers as he pushed her back against the rocks of the grotto, his hands on her breasts, crushing them deliciously beneath his palms, the taut nipples like hard buds as he nipped at them with his clever fingers.

'Pekhnidi mou,' he taunted, huskily soft, his mouth hot against her flesh as he traced a path down the long, vulnerable curve of her throat into the sensitive hollows of her shoulder. 'My sweet, sexy little plaything…'

This time she couldn't deny it—that was just what she was. A sudden wave of shame flooded through her. How could she have behaved with such utter wantonness? How could she be letting him do this to her?

But it was much too late now for second thoughts. For a moment her head swam dizzily, and then she realised that he had laid her down across the low rocks at the edge of the pool, and as she opened her eyes wide in shock he smiled down at her lazily, his hand sliding down over her naked body, asserting his right of possession over every slender inch.

A hot shiver ran through her at his touch. High above them the silver face of the moon sailed across a sky of velvet black; the hard edges of the rocks beneath her were bruising her back, but she couldn't protest—she could only surrender helplessly to whatever was going to happen.

His dark head bent over her breasts, and she felt the brush of his mouth against her skin as he dusted their aching swell with butterfly kisses. She closed her eyes, her head tipping back, losing herself in the sweet swirl of pleasure as his moist, sensuous tongue lapped across the ripe, tender bud of her nipple, his hard white teeth nipping at it teasingly, and she moaned softly as he drew it into his mouth, suckling at it with a deep, hungry rhythm that pulsed through her veins like a fever.

His hand was stroking slow circles over the smooth curve of her stomach, and then on down her slender thighs, slipping easily between them to coax them slightly apart. She submitted without resistance, her body arched back invitingly for him, and a soft sigh escaped her lips as he sought the most intimate caresses. Heat was pooling in the pit of her stomach like liquid gold as his exquisite touch explored the moist velvet folds, finding the tiny seed-pearl nestling within and wakening it to a sizzling arousal, his long fingers dipping deep inside her to warn her of the demand to come.

I love you. The words were whispered inside her head, but she held them back; she was giving him her body, defeated by a temptation that was just too much to withstand, but she wouldn't let him know that he had her heart as well. Perhaps he would guess, but she wouldn't confirm it—she had her pride.

She felt him shift his weight to lie above her, and she opened her eyes to watch him, breathing in deeply the musky scent of his skin, wanting to capture this moment in her memory and hold it for ever. For a brief moment she tensed, apprehensive as she sensed the raw male power he was still holding in check, but then, as she moved invitingly beneath him, he let go his breath in a ragged growl, and took her with one deep, hard thrust.

He wasn't gentle, but she didn't care. She melted against him, wrapping her arms around him, her whole body responding, drowning in the sweet, honeyed tide of sensuality that was sweeping through her veins. They moved together in some kind of erotic, primeval dance as ancient as Aphrodite herself, splashing in the shallow waters of her pool, bruising themselves heedlessly against the rocks, almost savage in their hunger for each other.

She could feel his heart pounding in a frenzied rhythm next to her own, feel the smooth movement of muscle beneath his damp skin as he thrust into her, wild and hard, taking his own pleasure but giving her more, and the heat inside her spiralled into a dizzying vortex of flame that lifted her higher and higher, until with a last, wild surge they both cried out, falling, falling, to land in an exhausted, breathless heap, washed up on the rocks beside the pool as the silver moon sailed on high above them.

It seemed like a long, long time later that Megan felt Theo moving, and it was a moment or two before she realised that he was laughing. She glared up at him, indignant.

'What's so funny?'

'This… Us! What a crazy thing to do.' He rolled off her, sprawling on the rocks beside her, a broad, triumphant grin on his face. 'We must both be covered in bruises, and we're damned lucky we didn't both drown!'

She sat up, curving her shoulder away from him in a somewhat belated attempt to preserve a little dignity. 'Well, it was your idea.'

He shook his head, his eyes glinting with mocking amusement. 'I never intended to let it go so far—I hadn't anticipated that you would be so delightfully wanton.

Oh, I'm not complaining,' he added, trailing his fingertip lazily down the length of her spine. 'What more could a man want in a mistress?'

His mistress... Only yesterday she had angrily insisted that she *wouldn't* be his mistress, but she had known even then that she would have no resistance when it came to the crunch. It shamed her a little to remember how easily she had surrendered; she had given him every reason to assume that he now had exactly what he wanted—a compliant little plaything willing to satisfy his physical needs whenever he felt bored with the tedium of his convenient marriage. Someone he could summon with a snap of his fingers, who would respond to his casual seduction as helplessly as she had tonight.

Some measure of pride reasserted itself, and she rose to her feet, going over to retrieve her discarded clothing. She couldn't be bothered to fiddle with her bra, but once she had her dress back on she felt a little less vulnerable, a little more able to confront him. 'Listen,' she asserted firmly, 'I'll...be your mistress—at least, until you marry Eleni. But let's get one thing absolutely clear. I am *not* your plaything, and I never will be. So don't call me that again—in English *or* in Greek!'

And with that she turned on her heel, and with as much dignity as she could muster she marched back to the car.

Megan awoke to the sweet chattering of a song-thrush. It sounded quite close, and opening one eye she saw that it was perched just outside the window, on the cedar-wood rail of a balcony that looked out over the tops of a forest of blue-green pine trees. For a fleeting moment she wondered what had happened to the sea... And then she remembered.

Turning her head on the pillow, she looked at the man still sleeping beside her, long black lashes shadowing his hard cheekbones, his black hair tousled, his wide chest naked above the sheet which had half slipped off the bed. A hunk, her old ward sister used to call him; what would she have said if she could have seen them now?

She suspected that Sally wouldn't really have envied her. Men like Theo Nikolaides were all very well to fantasise about, but it wasn't wise for an ordinary sort of girl like her to get too close. There was no way she could have prevented herself from falling in love with him, from winding up in his bed like this, even though she knew she was no more to him than a casual diversion; she would be lucky if she could hold his interest for more than a couple of days. To a man like him, sex was just an appetite to be satisfied, in the same way as hunger—and, if there didn't happen to be a gourmet meal available, he would make do with a snack of bread and butter until something more interesting came along.

With a small sigh she slipped out of bed, and padded barefoot over to the window to look out at the view. The house was in the mountains, high up on the southern slopes of the Troödos range, and below them the cedar forest fell away in a series of long valleys, the trees etched like lace against the drifting swirls of morning mist.

She hadn't known that Theo was planning to bring her here. After what had happened at Aphrodite's Pool, she had felt a little awkward when they had got back to the car, not knowing quite what to say to him. So to avoid conversation as they drove back along the coast she had feigned sleep—which had turned to genuine sleep at some point after they had left the sea behind.

She had woken only when the car had crunched to a halt on the driveway in front of the house. From the outside, she had seen a two-storey chalet built of cedar-wood, perched on a rocky spur, surrounded by forest; she had thought then that it was the prettiest house she had ever seen. But that hadn't meant she was willing to stay. She had argued vociferously, trying to insist that Theo drive her back down to the villa, but he had simply laughed at her, and then kissed her—and then made love to her over the bonnet of the car.

Her cheeks flamed red at the memory of how easily she had submitted to that swift, fierce demand as he had leaned her back over the still warm engine and slipped off her tiny lace briefs before she had even realised what he was going to do. Then he had simply scooped her up in his arms, and carried her into the house before she could find the strength to protest further.

He had brought her straight into this room, and dumped her in the middle of the bed. She had to admit that it was a much more comfortable place to make love, she mused now, a small, reminiscent smile curving her soft mouth as she glanced back at it over her shoulder, almost incredulous as she remembered the long night...

Two narrow glints of blue were smiling at her in amusement. 'You're up very early,' Theo remarked lazily.

'Habit,' she managed, suddenly a little breathless. 'I...don't usually sleep in. I usually have to go to work.'

'Well, not today,' he responded, hauling himself up against the pillows so that the sheet slipped even lower. 'Today you can stay in bed for as long as you like.'

She returned him a look of startled question. 'Aren't we going home?'

He laughed, shaking his head. 'There's no hurry. I

want you to myself for a few days—I want to be able to make love to you whenever I like, with no one else around to bother us.'

'A few days?' she protested, shocked. 'But... We can't stay up here all that time. What about Dakis?'

'Dakis will be fine—as he said, he's got a house full of staff to take care of him. And as for anyone else...it's none of their business.'

'It's Eleni's business,' she pointed out with a touch of asperity. 'You're supposed to be engaged to her, not...'

'Not spending a few days in the mountains with my mistress? I told you, Eleni knows the score. Besides, she's having a whale of a time, making her depredations on the shopping capitals of Europe. Come back to bed.'

She hesitated, struggling for some measure of self-restraint. She didn't like the way he could make her surrender so easily—he would learn to take her for granted. But with one swift, lithe movement he was across the room, catching her up and swinging her round—and she found herself thrown back across the bed, pinned beneath him, his laughing face inches above her own.

'It's a little late for maidenly reluctance, don't you think?' he taunted. 'I've had you at a world-famous tourist site, I've had you over the bonnet of a car—I had you in this bed last night more times than I bothered to count. But I haven't had enough of you yet—not nearly enough. I want you in every way there is.'

His mouth came down over hers, hot and enticing, but, summoning every ounce of will-power she possessed, she kept her lips firmly closed, her body stiff and unyielding. For a moment he persisted, but then he lifted his head, looking down at her in puzzled query.

'I told you last night that I won't be your plaything,' she asserted with grim determination.

'So...?'

'I...won't ask much of you,' she managed awkwardly. 'I don't expect you to fall in love with me or anything. But I do want some respect. I'm entitled to that, I think.'

He drew in a long, slow breath, and for a moment she thought that he was angry. But then he rolled over to lie beside her on the bed. 'Yes, you are,' he acknowledged, drawing her over on top of him. 'And I'm sorry if I made you feel as if I didn't respect you.' His hard mouth twisted into a crooked smile. 'It's a bad trait of mine, I'm afraid. I don't want to make excuses, but I probably inherited it from my father.'

His voice had taken on an acid note, and she frowned. 'From Dakis?'

He sighed, his blue eyes shadowed. 'He's treated women like chattels all his life—including my mother. I've stopped counting the number of affairs he's had. Even up to just a few years ago he was keeping a little redhead in an apartment in Limassol—and even then he wasn't faithful to her. He drove my mother almost demented with his womanising, though she put up with it for years—until finally it was too much, even for her, and she left him.'

'Why did she put up with it for so long?' she asked softly.

'Because she loved him.' He smiled without humour. 'The ironic thing is that she was probably the only one of his women who really did—the rest were mostly attracted by his money.'

'That's sad,' she murmured. 'He must have known in a way that he was short-changing himself with all those cheap affairs. Maybe that's why he had so many of them—he was always looking for something more, never even realising that he'd overlooked it right on his own doorstep. And now that he's old he's got no one to care about him. He's lonely.'

'He deserves it.'

'You don't mean that,' she protested, recognising the hurt behind his bitter words.

'No… Maybe I don't,' he acknowledged, shrugging his wide shoulders in a gesture of reluctant concession. 'Whatever he's been, he's still my father, I suppose.'

'So…are you going to do what he wants?' she asked, wary of provoking his annoyance. 'Stay here in Cyprus, and help him run the family business?'

'Probably.' He stroked his hand down the length of her spine, slowly, sensuously. 'Are you an angel, sent from heaven to bring out my better nature?' he teased.

'I'd like to think you could find your better nature yourself,' she admitted, her soft mouth curved into a wry smile. 'But as for being an angel…' She knelt up on the bed, straddled across him, the glint in her eyes far from angelic. 'I'm not sure about that.'

Last night had been incredible, but he had been the one in control. Now it was her turn. Slowly she let her fingertips trail down over his chest, curling into the rough, dark male hair that was scattered across it, feeling the resilience of hard muscle beneath his bronzed skin. He lay back on the bed, watching her, a glint of quizzical amusement in the narrowed blue slits of his eyes.

She took his mockery as a challenge. Several times during the long night of making love he had teased her, laughing at the way she responded so helplessly to his expert touch. Now she would have her revenge. Aphrodite, the goddess of love, would be her guide, lending her magical skills to torment him to within an inch of losing his sanity.

She began slowly. Her hands slid up over his wide chest again, circling over the thick bunch of muscles in his shoulders, and then on up the strong column of his neck to find the tiny spot just behind his ears which she had discovered last night could produce quite an interesting reaction.

She sensed the first warning tremor of arousal in him, and her mouth curved into a provocative smile. 'Patience,' she murmured, mimicking his teasing whisper of last night. She drew her fingertips down along the line of his hard jaw, her touch lighter than a butterfly's wing—down again over his throat and chest, reciting the names of the muscle groups as she went. 'Sterno-mastoid, pectoralis major, serratus anterior...'

'Is this a conducted tour?' he enquired with a touch of dry humour.

'I'm revising,' she responded mischievously. 'When I go back to England I may need to retrain if I decide to go in for community nursing. And you're a *very* good subject—your muscles are very well defined.'

'I'm glad that I can be of some use.'

Her eyes danced wickedly. 'Oh, that's not the only use I intend for you,' she purred. 'But I'm coming to that.'

'Good.'

Her fingertips continued their journey, trailing over the hard ridges of muscle down his stomach, but then, with a soft chuckle, she let them slide away, and, bending over him, she began instead to lay soft kisses along the hard line of his cheekbones, across his temples, down over his throat. He simply lay there, watching her, the blue gleam of his eyes inciting her to greater boldness.

This time she let her moist, hot mouth follow the same path her hands had taken. The musky, male scent of his skin was filling her senses, and she breathed it in deeply, feeling it stir the instinctive feminine responses inside her, heating her blood, making her heart beat faster.

Now she was letting the anticipation build, her hands and kisses roaming in a delicious exploration over every inch of his lean, hard body, thrilling to the powerful shudders of arousal that he couldn't suppress as, by every circuitous diversion she could invent, she approached slowly what they both knew was her goal.

Where had this wanton creature come from? She had never been aware that somewhere in the core of the sensible, professional person she had believed herself to be there was hidden a sensuality, an erotic imagination equal to that of any courtesan. It must be Aphrodite's influence, she mused fleetingly—whatever, it was a pretty potent spell.

She was enjoying this game, enjoying the sense of power as this strong man groaned in agonised pleasure as her tender caresses brought him to the peak of his arousal. And then she drew back a little, her eyes glittering sinfully beneath her lowered lashes as she teased him, returning again to use her soft mouth and hot, swirling tongue to drive him wild.

But she had no intention of neglecting her own pleasure, so just at the point where she sensed that the tension inside him was about to explode she drew back again, moving so that her body lay over his, and, with a long sigh of satisfaction, let herself yield to the penetrating hardness until he was deep, deep inside her.

The rhythm was hers, an erotic dance as she knelt over him, her slender hips circling and swaying, her body arched and her head tipped back, her own breathing ragged in her ears. Her temperature was rising, a fever in her blood, flames darting up the length of her spine, consuming her, until with one last, wild tremor she cried out, feeling him shudder beneath her, and she fell into his arms, both equally sated, equally exhausted, their sweat-slicked bodies tangled up in the sheets.

CHAPTER NINE

'KALIMERA, eromeni-mou.'

Megan glanced up with a smile, her heart giving a little skip of pleasure as Theo came down the steps of the terrace where she was finishing her breakfast. He came up behind her chair, leaning right over her and wrapping his arms around her so that his hands cupped intimately the firm swell of her breasts, and she tipped her head back into the crook of his shoulder.

'Missed me?' he murmured, his breath warm against her cheek.

'Yes,' she admitted simply, her lips parting invitingly as his mouth came down to claim hers in a lingeringly tender kiss, her spine arching as she leaned back into his embrace, her breasts aching for the pleasure of his caress—though at the same time she was conscious of a stab of anxiety that they might be seen.

He had been away for three days, in London. She knew he had seen Eleni while he was there, and she had tortured herself with jealousy, thinking about them together, wondering if he had told her the truth about his cold-blooded engagement. And even if he had there was still the possibility that there was someone else—one of the many girlfriends he had been linked with over the past few years, maybe, or someone he had just met, someone who could provide him with the excitement of a new conquest.

She had known it would be difficult. It was six weeks now since that incredible night at Aphrodite's Pool, when she had first become his mistress—six weeks when he had come every night to her room, often simply strolling casually down the corridor, increasingly careless of the need for discretion.

She had protested, but he had merely shrugged her concerns aside. 'Eleni isn't here,' he had declared. 'So why should it bother her?' It wasn't an argument that could quiet her conscience, but though she still felt the guilt of her position she had mostly given up worrying that the staff might be gossiping—after all, if he didn't care, why should she?

'How was your trip?' she queried, pouring him a cup of coffee.

'Not bad. I managed to tie up the agreement for the purchase of the Platres property.'

'That'll please Dakis. What did the bank make of it?'

'They liked it. Skiing is very popular now, and people are always looking for somewhere a little different.'

'Well, skiing in Cyprus will certainly be different!' Megan acknowledged with a laugh. 'Did you fly back yourself?'

He shook his head. 'I took a scheduled flight—the Lear needed a check on the port engine. Are those croissants still warm?' He reached for the plate. 'I had breakfast on the plane, but that was a couple of hours ago.'

'And…how was London?' she enquired tentatively—that was as close as she cared to get to asking him about his fiancée.

He shrugged those wide shoulders in a gesture that indicated there was little of interest to report. 'Enjoying a bit of a heatwave. Everyone's out in their shirt-sleeves, and getting sunburned.'

She laughed, relaxing in the glorious warmth of the reliable Mediterranean sun that had tanned her slim body to a lightly toasted golden brown, and lightened her hair to almost white. 'They have to make the most of it,' she remarked with a detached sympathy. 'It won't last.'

'No.' He smiled, a slow, sensuous smile, as his eyes slid with unmistakable appreciation over her slender legs, which were stretched out with her feet propped on the walled edging of one of the flowerbeds. 'Mmm—I do like those shorts,' he remarked teasingly. 'They're so very…short.' He reached across to stroke his hand up the length of her thigh.

'Theo…!' she protested, glancing up swiftly towards the house. 'Someone might see us.'

'So…?'

He leaned closer, burying his teeth in her bare shoulder and nipping lightly, leaving a circle of faint red marks against her golden skin. His hand continued upwards, over the few inches of bare midriff that showed above her shorts, to seek teasingly beneath the edge of the sleeveless white shirt she had tied beneath her breasts.

'All the time I was stuck in London I was cursing the wasted nights when I could have been making love to you,' he murmured, his voice taking on a husky timbre. 'All I could think about was your lovely body, and the things I wanted to be doing to you…'

'Theo, don't…'

It was a weak protest, which he ignored. His hand stroked over the ripe swell of her breast, lingering caressingly, and then slipped inside her shirt, beneath the Lycra of her bikini-top, to fondle the warm, naked flesh, toying with the tender bud of her nipple until it tautened into a pert pink peak.

'"Theo, don't"?' he mocked playfully. 'You know you don't want me to stop.'

To her shame, that was all too true—she never knew how to resist him. It took him only seconds to reduce her to a state of helpless rapture, all thought of anyone who might be watching them forgotten as his mouth came down to claim hers, his languorous tongue swirling over the delicate membranes of her lips, expertly igniting her responses.

She had fought for his respect, and most of the time she felt she was having some success; though the flames of their physical attraction burned as fiercely as ever, the time they spent making love was balanced by time just talking. He would tell her about Cyprus—its long history, his concern to balance the demands of the tourist-led economy with the urgent need to preserve the island's delicate eco-system. And he would listen as she talked about her job, showing a genuine interest, proud of her achievement in gaining so much responsibility so quickly.

But sometimes—as now—the old arrogant, demanding Theo would resurface to reassert the primitive order of the predatory male and submissive female. And, though she had no intention of admitting it, she secretly enjoyed those moments—moments when she could let herself surrender to her deepest instincts, let herself believe that loving him was enough, that there was no tomorrow, no Eleni, nothing beyond the sensual darkness swirling around them like a warm velvet cloak...

The sound of footsteps—slightly unsteady footsteps still—warned them of Dakis's approach. Reluctantly Theo sat back, adopting an air of cool insouciance as if nothing had been happening, as Megan fumbled with numb fingers to retie the loosened knot of her shirt, her cheeks a blaze of scarlet.

But if Dakis noticed anything amiss he gave no sign

of it. 'Ah, there you are, *iyos mou*! Anna said you were home. How was your trip? Everything is settled?' He came carefully down the steps—he had obstinately refused to continue using his cane, insisting that he could now manage without it—and settled himself on one of the other chairs. 'You have completed the purchase? The bank have agreed our terms?'

'It's all in hand, Papa,' Theo responded, his tone deliberately calm in contrast to his father's excitability. 'I've left them to go over the figures.'

'What's the problem?' Dakis demanded fiercely. 'It's all there in the proposal! They'll get a first-class return on their investment. What more do they want?'

'It *is* a big investment, Papa,' Theo reminded him gently. 'Of course they need time to consider it.'

'Hah! Bankers! They're nothing but a flock of sheep! They wouldn't know a good investment if it came up and bit their noses off! Oh, I wish I could have gone myself—I'd have told them a thing or two about how to make money.'

'I'm quite sure you would, Papa,' Theo responded with admirable patience. 'But if you want me to be involved you have to trust me to do things in my own way.'

Dakis scowled, but he had learned over the past few weeks not to waste his energy arguing too much with his son. 'All right,' he conceded grudgingly. 'Just tell me all about it.'

'Later, Papa,' Theo insisted, rising easily to his feet. 'I've only just got back—I could do with a shower.' His blue eyes slanted a flickering glance towards Megan, and she could read the meaning in them as plainly as if he had spoken; he had rather more interesting things on his mind than washing away the dust of his journey.

'Will you be long?' Dakis demanded, his thoughts only on business.

'Not long. Say, an hour?'

Megan stood up too. 'I...just remembered there's something I have to...tell Anna,' she announced, hoping Dakis wouldn't notice the betraying tremor in her voice. 'I'll see you in a little while.' And, taking her book, she followed Theo up the terrace steps.

The house was cool after the fierce heat of the Mediterranean sun—usually, Dakis had told her, he would go up to the chalet in the mountains for the summer months, but he would have found it difficult to manage all the stairs. Megan was secretly quite glad of that; she preferred to keep the memory of the chalet, and her time there with Theo, intact.

She glanced up at him now a little shyly. She had hardly dared hope that his interest in her would last so long, but it seemed undiminished. And as the weeks had passed her own feelings had deepened; what had started as a powerful physical attraction had grown and changed, as she had come to know the real man inside the 'hunk' that had so dazzled her friend Sally. Loving him had become part of her, as deep as her bones and sinews—something that would be part of her for as long as she lived.

The smile he gave her made her heart flip over. 'Your place or mine?' he enquired with sinful humour.

'I...don't know if we should,' she demurred, glancing nervously along the passage. 'It's broad daylight...'

'I've been away three whole days,' he growled hungrily. 'I want to make love to you right now.' And, without allowing her any further time for argument, he swung her up into his arms, tossing her into the air and catching her again as if she weighed nothing at all, and strode off down the passage to his own rooms, at the end of the west wing of the house.

She had been here a few times, briefly, but she had not yet been right inside. He had kept it very simple, almost stark—the floor was panelled in cedar-wood, and the walls were plain white, hung with three massive bas-relief plaster panels—copies, she knew, of panels found in the ancient temples. The principal focus of the room was a sleekly sculptural Bang & Olufsen hi-fi system that looked as if it could guide a manned space-flight, set between two vast leather-upholstered sofas. But he didn't linger here, carrying her straight through to the bedroom.

This too was very plain. The bed was wide and low to the floor, covered with a spread of dark blue hand-loomed wool. Beside it was a wicker table, with a reading lamp and a stack of books, and by the window that opened out to the balcony were a wicker armchair and another table, also stacked with books. Above the bed was a mosaic—another copy from one of the temples. Her eyes widened as she gazed at it.

'What exactly are they *doing*?' she queried.

He chuckled. 'Can't you work it out?'

'Well...yes,' she admitted. 'But I'm not sure that it's anatomically possible—not unless they're both double-jointed!'

'We could always try it out,' he suggested, letting her slide down his body to land on her tiptoes, still held close against him.

She shook her head decisively. 'One of us would probably put our back out. I suspect there's an element of artistic licence there.'

'Spoilsport,' he murmured, his voice taking on a huskier timbre as his mouth came down to meet hers.

Their bodies were so attuned to each other that each time they made love it was better than the last. Sometimes it would be swift, fuelled by frenzy, while at other times—as now—it was long and slow and tender—warm, intimate kisses and soft, lingering caresses, each of them knowing how best to give the other pleasure, losing themselves in mindless bliss, with no thought or consciousness beyond the dark velvet boundaries of their private, sensual world.

Afterwards, as they lay wrapped up in each other's arms, Theo sighed with satisfaction, nuzzling into her neck. 'Mmm—I'd forgotten how delicious you smell.'

She laughed in lazy contentment. 'I suppose we ought to get up...?' she suggested reluctantly.

'Uh-uh.' Theo shook his head, drawing her close in against him so that they were nestled together like two spoons in a drawer. 'What's the hurry? I could stay here all day.'

Yes, she could too—she could stay here for ever... But that was impossible, a small, niggling voice whispered inside her head. Dakis was almost fully recovered, and soon her contract would be coming to an end. And Theo... Theo would be marrying Eleni.

With an effort of will, she detached herself from his embrace, and rolled off the bed, walking over to the wide full-length windows that opened onto his private balcony, and the view of the sea. It was strange to think that in just a few weeks she would be back in England, soon to be shrouded in the dismal grey of autumn—strange that there would be no more of these clear, vivid blue skies, the endless sunshine, the soft whisper of waves against the shore...

Tears were stinging at the back of her eyes, and she

tried to blink them back, but a single one spilled over, and began to track slowly down her cheek.

Theo had slid off the bed, and followed her across the room. 'You're crying,' he accused now, taking her insistently into his arms. 'Why are you crying?'

'Oh, just…' The soft note of concern in his voice was almost too much for her. 'I just… I was just thinking about how much I shall miss all this when I've gone. The sea, the sunshine…'

'Then don't go,' he argued, drawing her closer to him. 'Stay here.'

'I can't,' she protested, shaking her head. 'My contract is nearly finished—Dakis doesn't need me any more…'

'*I* need you.'

She lifted her eyes to gaze up at him, but shook her head, her soft mouth curved into a small, wistful smile. 'No,' she asserted sadly. 'We've had fun, but…neither of us had the intention of it lasting very long.'

He laughed, gently mocking her. 'You're a terrible liar, *poulaki mou*,' he teased. 'Do you think that I don't know you're in love with me?'

She caught her breath, startled. 'I…never said that…'

'You didn't need to,' he murmured, dropping a light kiss on the tip of her nose. 'Your eyes tell me—and your body, every time we make love. And it was me you saw when you looked into Aphrodite's Pool that night, wasn't it?'

She nodded, unable to deny it. A small sob escaped her lips, and she buried her face in the hard wall of his chest, breathing in with a kind of desperation the familiar musky scent of his skin. She loved him so much, even though she knew she couldn't have him; she had fought a constant battle with herself, but she was glad now, in a way, that he knew—it was almost like a kind of leaving present.

He tilted up her chin, forcing her to look at him. 'You weren't the only one who looked into Aphrodite's Pool that night,' he murmured huskily. 'And who do you think I saw?'

She stared up at him, her heart fluttering against her ribs, hardly daring to believe what she was hearing. But the message in his eyes seemed to give her the answer—and as his lips brushed over hers she heard him whisper softly, 'It wasn't supposed to happen...'

She melted into his kiss, closing her mind to the niggling voice of reason, refusing to question a dream so fragile that she feared it would blow away like dust. He was in love with her—he was really in love with her. There would be no end to this happiness—it would last for ever...

A sharp rap at the door startled them both.

'Damn!' For a moment Theo seemed inclined to ignore it, but a second rap, more urgent, warned that whoever it was wasn't going to go away. Slanting Megan a wry smile, he reluctantly let her go. 'Don't go away— I'll be back in a minute.' He reached for the navy blue silk dressing gown that hung on a hook behind the door, shrugging into it and tying the belt as he walked through the sitting room of the suite and over to the door.

But Megan's guilty conscience wouldn't let her be so cool about it. Hurriedly she snatched up her clothes from where they had been discarded beside the bed, and darted into the bathroom, her heart pounding. Had Eleni been warned about what was going on? Had she returned to accuse them? Her fuddled mind could think of no plausible excuse to explain what she was doing in

Theo's room, but once she was properly dressed again she felt at least a little better.

But as she cautiously opened the bathroom door Theo strode back into the bedroom, his face pale and taut.

'What's the matter?' she asked anxiously.

'It's Papa—he's collapsed.' He had already thrown off his dressing gown, and was grabbing for a shirt. 'They've rung for an ambulance.'

Megan stared at him in cold horror. 'Oh, my God—not another stroke?'

He nodded grimly. 'It looks like it. He's in the study.'

'I'll go down.'

It wasn't the moment to worry about anyone seeing her leaving Theo's room. She raced down the passage, almost falling over her own feet in her hurry to get down the stairs. Several of the domestic staff were standing around the doorway to the study, but they moved aside as she came to the door, their faces grave.

Dakis was on the floor. His face was so grey that for one dreadful moment she thought he was dead, but then she heard the dry rasp as he dragged in a shallow breath and let it go in a rough sigh. She knelt beside him, feeling for his pulse, but there was nothing she could do for him at the moment except make him comfortable.

'Should we lift him onto the sofa?' It was Ioannis, Dakis's valet, his voice a tense whisper.

Megan shook her head. 'But help me turn him onto his side, and give me a couple of cushions.'

It was Theo who helped her—he must have dressed in record time—and as they settled his father carefully on the cushions he glanced up at her, concern etched into his face. 'How bad is it?' he asked.

'It's impossible to say,' she responded, desperately wishing she could be more optimistic. 'He's breathing, at least. The important thing is to get him to hospital. If he survives the first few days…' She couldn't restrain herself from reaching out her hand and squeezing his, just for a brief moment—it really made no difference at the moment what people might read into such a gesture.

It seemed like an eternity that they waited for the ambulance, but in truth it could only have been a few minutes. One of the maids had been sent to the front door to let the ambulancemen in, and Megan sighed with relief as she watched them lift Dakis gently onto a stretcher, knowing that within a short time he would be safely at the hospital.

'You ride in the ambulance with him,' Theo suggested. 'I'll follow in my car.'

She nodded, taking Dakis's hand as the stretcher was carried carefully to the front door and down the steps. There were tears in her eyes, but she didn't bother to brush them away. It had been such a shock. He had seemed to be so well—there had been no warning that another stroke was pending. But he was a fighter, she reminded herself, clinging to any shred of hope—he would get over this one as he had the first one.

She squeezed his hand tightly as the ambulance started up. 'Hold on, Dakis,' she pleaded softly through her tears. 'Don't give in. You can make it—I know you can.'

It seemed a little strange to be in a hospital but not be part of the staff. The only real difference between this hospital and any Megan had known in England, apart from the constant bright sunshine streaming in through the windows, was that all the signs were written in Greek as well as English. But they were the same signs, tugging at her with their familiarity: 'Casualty', 'Pathology', 'Outpatients' Clinic'...

Dakis had been put in a private room that looked out over a quiet, leafy courtyard bathed in golden afternoon sunshine, but he was in no condition to appreciate the view. He lay with closed eyes, his face almost the same colour as the pillow, but Megan was relieved to see that the green trace on the heart monitor was regular, if a little weak, and his breathing seemed rather less laboured than it had a few hours ago.

A nurse had just finished taking his blood pressure, and she gave them a reassuring smile. 'That's not too bad—he's holding his own. The doctor will be round again as soon as we have the results of the cat scan.'

Theo nodded, watching the old man for any sign of response. Megan, who had moved from her chair to let the nurse get close to the bed, sat down again. Theo glanced at her, his smile a little crooked. 'Thank you.'

'For what?'

'Oh...just for being here.' He sighed, a little awkward as he put his hand over the thin parchment-like one on the bed. 'I wish I knew whether he knows we're here.'

'He can probably hear you,' she assured him quietly. 'Just keep talking to him—it doesn't matter what about.'

Theo shrugged, and leaned forward, frowning as he sought in his mind for something to say. 'Papa, do you remember when I was small, and you taught me to ski, up on Mount Olympus? Some years there was enough snow that we could even go cross-country skiing, and you used to say that one day you'd take me to Canada, where we could go heli-skiing.'

He talked on, rambling reminiscences of his child-hood, and Megan sat quietly and watched. Dakis gave little sign of responding, but there seemed to be more of a look of tranquillity on his face. The soft plink-plink of the heart monitor was a counterpoint to Theo's voice, and Megan smiled to herself, her gaze wandering out to the leaf-shaded courtyard.

The first few hours had been tense, but, having survived the first crisis, there were at least some grounds for hoping that Dakis would continue to improve. But, whatever happened, at least in the last few weeks he and his son had managed to bury the long-standing enmity that had lain between them. It was sad that it had taken a serious illness for them both to lower the prickly barrier of pride, but in that, as in so many other things, they were two of a kind.

The minutes ticked quietly away as outside the normal bustle of a busy hospital continued. Megan was half dozing when a sudden commotion outside jerked her abruptly awake; she heard the unmistakable—and unwelcome—voice of Dakis's nephew Giorgos. There was a brief moment for Megan to exchange a wry look with Theo, and then the door opened and he stalked into the room, his sour-faced wife at his side.

On the threshold he paused, his piggy eyes focused on Megan in icy disdain, before turning to Theo. *'Kalispera, Ksaderfos Theo,'* he greeted him coldly.

'Good evening, Cousin Giorgos,' Theo returned, his own voice laced with mocking sarcasm. 'How dutifully prompt you are in attendance on my father. Though only what I would have expected of you, of course.'

Giorgos's lip curled, and he answered in Greek, his tone loftily sanctimonious.

'How kind of you to say so,' Theo responded, his smile lacking any hint of warmth. 'Fortunately he seems to be holding on, as you can see. In a few days, no doubt, he'll be sitting up and shouting at all the nurses.'

'Hah!' Giorgos slanted an evil look towards Megan. 'That will no doubt be a disappointment to your little *poutana*,' he sneered.

Megan bridled; she wasn't entirely sure what the word meant, but she could guess that it wasn't complimentary. But Theo intervened on her behalf.

'Such language from your refined lips, my dear cousin?' he countered, a sardonic inflection in his voice. 'I'm surprised it's even in your vocabulary.'

Giorgos laughed harshly. 'No other word would be quite so appropriate. You think I do not know what has been going on? You are both great fools, you and your father. How will you feel when he leaves all his money to that…creature?'

Theo arched one dark eyebrow in quizzical amusement. 'You think that's likely?'

It was Giorgos's turn to adopt a sardonic tone. 'You mean you do not know of the new disposition he has made of his affairs?' he queried loftily. 'It was completed while you were in London. Everything goes to her—every penny. If you do not believe me, enquire of his lawyers—they will confirm that it is so.'

'Papa's made a new will?' Theo frowned sharply, shooting a questioning glance towards Megan. 'Did you know about this?'

She stared at him, aghast. 'Of course I didn't know! How could you even think I would?'

Giorgos crowed. 'Such innocence! But of course she would deny it—what would you expect? She has seduced you, flaunting her body to blind you to her schemes. And now she sits here, with such pretended concern, while all the time she is counting the moments until she can begin to spend your father's money.'

Megan was so stunned by the accusation that she was

having difficulty forming any coherent response. But as she looked to Theo, expecting him to assume her defence, she was chilled to see the glint of anger in his blue eyes.

'Is this true?' he demanded tautly. 'Did I get it wrong? Was it all some kind of double bluff? Did you set out to make a fool of me from the beginning?'

'You can *believe* that?' She shook her head slowly, more to clear it of what seemed to be a nightmare than in denial of Giorgos's words—they should need no denial. Her fragile dream had shattered more quickly than even she had believed possible. Unsure that her legs would bear her weight, she rose to her feet. 'Well, if that's the case, there…doesn't seem very much point in my staying here,' she ground out, her voice shaking. 'Goodbye, Theo.'

Somehow she made it across the room, and out to the corridor. It was there that Theo caught up with her, catching her arm in a vice-like grip and turning her round. 'Answer me! Did you know? Has Giorgos been right about you all along?'

Gathering up every ounce of dignity she possessed, she met his eyes with a look of frosty contempt. 'You think I was sleeping with you, and at the same time schmoozing your father into changing his will in my favour?' she demanded. 'I feel sorry for you. Somewhere along the line you should have learned about love, and about trust, but you didn't. So you've ended up thinking everyone is the same as you—only interested in using people. I should have known *that* from the beginning, but I was the fool. I was in love with you. But I'll get over it.'

And, shaking off his grip on her arm, she turned and walked on down the corridor, half-blinded by tears that she refused to let him see her brush away.

CHAPTER TEN

'MEGAN?'

Megan recognised the low, slightly husky voice at once, and slammed the phone down without even hesitating. In the three days since she had returned home she had been on tenterhooks in case Theo should try to contact her—she had even extracted a promise from a bemused and sympathetic Cathy that she would deny any knowledge of her whereabouts if he should show up.

It was only her anger that had sustained her as she had left the hospital in Limassol. She had got a taxi back to the villa, asked the driver to wait, and then, after packing all her things at record speed, she had had him drive her straight to the airport. She had been lucky to find a vacant seat on a flight at the height of the season—she had had to change planes in Munich, but she would have happily travelled via Moscow if it would have got her off the island.

She had told herself over and over, in the sternest tones, that she didn't want him to follow her. Whether it was true or not that Dakis had changed his will she had no idea—though she couldn't imagine why he would have done anything so bizarre. But that was really beside the point. Theo should have known, without even having to ask her, that Giorgos's accusations were entirely malicious. If he loved her—as he had started to tell her—he should have known.

Cathy wandered into the room, yawning—it wasn't yet eleven o'clock, an unusually early hour for her to get up. 'Who was that on the phone?' she enquired vaguely.

Megan kept her head buried in the copy of *Nursing Times* she was reading. 'Wrong number,' she lied.

'Oh… Drat—there aren't any cornflakes. Be a love and get some if you go out later, would you? By the way, have you seen my yellow blouse…?'

'The silk one? It's in the hall.'

'How did it get there?' Cathy wandered out to retrieve the garment. 'Damn, there's a button missing, and I wanted to wear it tonight. We've got a gig at the Tramshed. Why don't you come along? You'll enjoy it—better than sitting indoors moping, anyway.'

'I'm not moping,' Megan protested.

Cathy shrugged. 'Call it what you like—it looks like moping to me. The trouble with you is, you take men too seriously. First there was boring old Jeremy…'

'I didn't know you thought Jeremy was boring,' Megan remarked, surprised.

'Well, I was hardly going to say as much when you were engaged to him, was I?' her sister countered dryly. 'But it was the best thing you ever did, dumping him. Now there's this Greek chap. I grant you he's dishy, but no man's worth making yourself miserable over. Forget him—go out and find yourself another one. In fact, find yourself more than one. Men are like goldfish—it's always better to have two or three swimming around in a bowl at the same time.'

Megan couldn't help but laugh at her sister's remark. 'Well, thank you for that advice on the science of fish-keeping,' she declared. 'And as for tonight—yes, I'd like to come. Even though I'm not moping!'

Maybe Cathy was right. Maybe she should go out and try to enjoy herself—though the way she felt at the moment a noisy evening at one of the way-out nightclubs where her sister's band tended to play was the last thing she wanted. But at least if Theo came looking for her he wouldn't find her sitting around waiting for him.

Unfortunately, Theo found her as she returned from the shops in Cathy's car. She had walked round to open the boot to get the shopping out when he suddenly appeared at her side. 'Hello, Megan,' he said quietly.

Her hand jerked sharply, scratching the paintwork with the key. 'Damn! Look what you made me do!'

He smiled, that warm, intimate smile that had once been able to melt all her resistance. 'I'm sorry…'

But as he moved a step towards her she stiffened, her eyes flashing him a warning not to come too close. 'Well, what do you want?' she demanded belligerently.

'I…just want to talk to you,' he responded, a little taken aback by her reaction. 'Could we go for a drink or something?'

'No, we couldn't.' The only defence she had was cold hostility. 'I don't have anything to say to you, and there's nothing you could say to me that I'd want to hear.'

He frowned, not accustomed to finding that his charm was not having its usual effect. 'Dakis…sends you his best regards.'

'Oh?' She turned away from him to open the boot of the car. Predictably, the shopping bags had tipped over, giving her the excuse of gathering up the spilled contents so that she didn't have to look at Theo. 'I'm glad to hear he's getting better.'

'He's still quite poorly. But he's well enough to talk. He…told me why he changed his will.'

She had to reach right into the corner of the boot to

retrieve a tin of tomato soup that had rolled away. 'Did he?' she queried, injecting a note of cool indifference into her voice.

'He was trying to force my hand,' Theo explained with an inflection of dry humour. 'He wanted me to marry you.'

Megan laughed, letting her bitterness show. 'I didn't realise his stroke had affected his sanity so badly,' she countered, lifting the shopping out of the boot and slamming the lid.

Theo shook his head, his smile crooked. 'He's not insane,' he responded, his eyes warm as they gazed down into hers. 'He's just an interfering old goat. But, as it happens, he had no need to meddle anyway. I want to marry you.'

She spat out a most unladylike expletive, and turned away from him, hefting the shopping bags into her arms and stalking across the car park towards the alley that led round to the front door of the apartment block.

Theo moved swiftly to block her path, his expression an amalgam of a dozen emotions. 'I mean it,' he asserted forcefully. 'I'm in love with you.'

'Oh, really?' she sneered, holding the shopping bags in front of her like a shield. 'And what does your fiancée think about that?'

He made a dismissive gesture with his hand. 'Eleni and I never had any intention of getting married,' he declared. 'The engagement was a convenience to both of us. Eleni wanted to break free of her family's excessive domination, and it was a useful opportunity for me to demonstrate to my father that I wouldn't tolerate him trying to manipulate me.'

She arched one eyebrow in cool enquiry. 'That may have been your intention, but I don't believe it was hers.

I saw the way she used to look at you—she was planning to stick to you like superglue.'

He conceded a wry smile. 'Well, maybe she did initially have some idea that she could have it both ways,' he acknowledged. 'But she soon changed her mind when I made it perfectly clear that while I was prepared to be an accommodating fiancé I would have been a very authoritarian husband. She's quite happy now—she's using the excuse of our broken engagement to enjoy an extended stay with some cousins in New York, where she's taking the shops by storm!'

'Well, bully for her,' Megan snapped acidly. 'Now, will you please get out of my way? This shopping's heavy.'

'Let me help you with it…'

'No!' She stepped back sharply as he reached for the bags. 'Just go away—leave me alone. I don't want anything more to do with you.'

'But I'm asking you to marry me…' he insisted, his voice aching with the confusion of someone who had always got exactly what he wanted, and couldn't believe that he was being refused.

'Big deal!' Her eyes were sparking angry fire. 'I'm afraid you're a little too late. Do you seriously think I'd even consider marrying you, when you believe I could be capable of the things your charming cousin was accusing me of?'

'Megan, I'm sorry. I don't blame you for being angry…'

'"Sorry" doesn't cut it.' She saw a gap between him and the wall, and darted through it before he had time to stop her, gripping her shopping and shaking him off as he tried to catch her arm.

'Megan, listen to me…'

'No. I hate you.' Tears were starting to sting her eyes, and she was desperate to get away from him before they started to fall. 'You made me be your mistress...'

'I don't recall that there was much coercion involved,' he countered on a sardonic note.

'You know what I mean,' she threw at him, furious. 'You lied to me about marrying Eleni—you let me think I was just some...trivial affair, your bit on the side.'

'And that hurt your pride?'

'Too right it did! You flaunted your pride at me— well, you're not the only one who can have pride. I have some too—too much to accept your generous offer of matrimony. So goodbye. Go back to Cyprus—go wherever you damned well like! Leave me alone to get on with my life. I never want to see you again. Ever.'

The doorbell rang next morning when Megan was in the bath. 'I'll get it,' Cathy carolled from her bedroom.

'No!' Scrambling out of the tub, Megan grabbed for a towel. 'No, don't answer it,' she pleaded urgently.

Her sister slanted her a look of wry impatience. 'You don't even know who it is,' she pointed out. 'It might be the postman.'

Megan's lips compressed. Dammit, why did Cathy have to choose to get up early today? 'Okay,' she conceded warily. 'But if it's...someone for me I'm not here.'

'You mean if it's a gorgeous Greek millionaire?' Her sister sighed, shaking her head. 'Why don't I get that lucky—to have a dish like that chasing me halfway across Europe? You wouldn't catch *me* slamming the door in his face!'

'Please, Cathy. I've done it often enough for you. Just say I'm not here.'

'All right,' Cathy agreed, smiling. 'You're not here.'

Megan slipped back into the bathroom and closed the door, leaving just a tiny crack so that she could hear what was being said. It wasn't the postman, anyway. Cathy was trying to make excuses, her voice apologetic—and totally lacking in conviction. Then she heard a laugh that was all too familiar.

'You're as useless at telling lies as she is,' Theo teased, laughing. 'Come on, Cathy, let me in—I know she's there.'

'Honestly, she's not… No…wait…!' Cathy's voice rose to a squeak, and Megan heard determined footsteps in the hall. With a stifled gasp she shut the bathroom door and bolted it, but he must have spotted the movement, and in seconds he was there, banging on the flimsy panels as she backed away, her eyes wide with horror as if she was expecting him to break it down.

'Megan? Come on, open the door,' he said insistently. 'I just want to talk to you.'

'I told you last night, it's too late for that,' she slammed back at him, a note of hysteria in her voice. 'Go away—you're wasting your time. I never want to see you again.'

'Megan, please. I never meant to hurt you. I love you. Just open the door…'

She had screwed up her fists, bunching them against her eyes, only glad that he couldn't see the state she was in. 'If you don't go away, I'll tell Cathy to call the police,' she warned him fiercely.

'Oh, come on,' he protested, laughing a little uncertainly. 'There's no need to do that.'

'Yes, there is,' she asserted, fuelling her anger to bolster her defences. 'And I will if you don't stop pestering me.'

There was a long pause, and then she heard his voice again, soft with regret. 'Was I really that bad?'

She closed her eyes tightly, struggling not to let herself succumb to the weakness that was washing through her. But she only had to conjure up the image of his eyes, looking at her with that cold, angry suspicion. 'It's too late, Theo,' she responded wearily. 'It's over—gone, dead, no more... It wouldn't have worked out anyway.'

'You know that's not true,' he countered, his voice low and urgent. 'We can't just leave it like this—I love you too much just to let you go.'

'I'm not going to talk to you, Theo,' she insisted. She could argue, tell him that love could never harbour the kind of suspicions he had felt about her, but there was no point. 'It's too late.'

'Megan, please...'

She sat down on the edge of the bath, watching the door with nervous eyes in case he tried to smash the flimsy bolt. But she didn't really think he would. If she just sat here long enough, refusing to answer him, eventually he would go away. He was too proud to plead for long.

But even so, when she heard him move away from the door, heard him talking quietly to Cathy, it was all she could do not to wrench the door open and throw herself into his arms. At last she heard the front door close, and a moment later Cathy tapped tentatively on the door.

'Megan? He's gone.'

Reluctantly she got up, and went over to unbolt the door. Cathy took one look at her tear-soaked face and wrapped her arms around her. 'Oh, Sis! You are a fool! Why on earth did you send him away like that, if you're going to cry about it?'

'It's a long story, Cathy—a very long story. And I have an appointment with the nursing agency about a job this afternoon—I have to get ready. I'll tell you about it this evening.'

'All right,' her sister conceded reluctantly. 'But I think you're mad. He's absolutely gorgeous, and he's in love with you. What more can you want than that?'

Megan sighed. 'My self-respect.'

She sent the roses back to the florist. The gift packages she refused to accept from the postman. She wouldn't take the telephone calls, and when she saw his car outside the flat she would walk on round the block, waiting for over an hour in the coffee-bar in the high street until she saw him drive away.

Cathy was sympathetic, if uncomprehending, and at work she managed to concentrate sufficiently to avoid any potentially dangerous mistakes, but she was like a walking zombie. At last, in a card that Cathy insisted on opening for her, he expressed his final regrets, and told her that he would be returning to Cyprus permanently.

After that, there was nothing but emptiness. She kept the card—she had thrown it away at first, but had retrieved it before the dustmen came, smoothing out the creases with hands that shook, barely able to see what she was doing for the tears that misted her eyes. And she had the photographs from that sunny morning above the rocky cove where Aphrodite was supposed to have been born from the foam of the sea.

The weeks passed, each one seeming like a thousand years. Summer gave way to a grey, dismal autumn, perfectly in keeping with Megan's mood. She moved out of Cathy's flat, into a tiny bedsitter that cost almost half her wages—though at least the money she had earned in

Cyprus had meant that she'd been able to clear her over-draft. And she had found out the details about retraining as a community nurse, but she hadn't had the motivation to apply.

And then one afternoon, just a few weeks before Christmas, as she hurried home from the bus stop, she was halted in her tracks by the past she had thought to be two thousand miles away. For a moment she hesitated—but even huddled beneath an umbrella she couldn't pretend not to have noticed a silver Rolls-Royce parked right outside her front door. As she drew level with it, the chauffeur jumped smartly out and opened the back door wide.

'Forgive me for not getting out,' came Dakis's voice from the back seat. 'I'm afraid it is still a little difficult for me.'

'Dakis?' She stepped up to the car, reluctantly accepting his invitation to join him as he patted the leather upholstery beside him. 'How are you?'

'Better than I was,' he acknowledged, gesturing to the chauffeur to close the door. 'Probably as good as I can hope to get, my doctors advise me.'

'You can walk?' she queried with genuine interest.

'Not very far. And my hand, regrettably, is of little use. But it will do.' He smiled with wry humour. 'It is better than the alternative.'

'Well, I'm…glad to see you looking so well, anyway.'

He regarded her with those gleaming dark eyes, still as bright as ever. 'You have cut your hair,' he remarked.

'Yes…' She touched her hand to the layered bob, now tousled by the wind. 'I finally managed to grow all that dreadful bleached stuff out.'

'I like it,' he approved, nodding. 'It has elegance.'

She laughed. 'Well, not at the moment—it needs a

comb through it. But at least I don't look like a tart any more.'

Her last words came out more bitter than she had intended, and there was a long, awkward silence. There were so many things that Megan wanted to ask him: where was Theo? What was he doing? Had he married Eleni after all? But part of her mind was arguing that it was better not to know. It was Dakis who spoke first.

'I was very sorry you left,' he said softly.

She sat gazing down at her hands, still holding the handle of the umbrella that was dripping a slow pool onto the carpet. 'I'm sorry I didn't stay to say goodbye, or to work out my contract, but…I had to go.'

'I know.' His voice was sad. 'My son told me what had happened. I…must tell you that I very much regret my part in it. I wanted him to marry, to bring me grandchildren, but he seemed only to choose to spend his time with those pretty little nothings, who would make big eyes at him, and coo over every word he uttered. Such a one would not do for him as a wife—he needs a woman who could make him respect her.'

'So you picked on me?'

He nodded. 'Exactly! You are perfect for him—I knew it from when first I met you. And I suspected that his interest could easily be aroused—I had seen him watch you as you were on the ward, and before I even mentioned you he asked me questions about you.'

'Did he?' Megan queried, startled.

'Indeed. And so I formed the idea of having you come to Cyprus, so that he would have the chance to come to know you.'

'But instead he got engaged to Eleni,' she remarked dryly.

'Hah! I knew from the start that was nothing but a

sham—did I not say so? I could see that his interest in you was growing—I do not care to listen to servants' gossip, but they said that he came every night to your room.'

Megan felt her cheeks blush faintly pink.

Dakis chuckled. 'I told you, he has very good taste, my son. But with my health I was becoming anxious, impatient—there could have been too little time. So I had the idea of changing my will so that everything would be left to you—I hoped that thus I could bring him to acknowledge what I was sure he truly felt. It was my intention only to use it as a weapon, you understand—to force his hand.'

She slanted him a crooked smile. 'Unfortunately it backfired on you.'

'Indeed it did.' He sighed heavily. 'I should have known better than to try to interfere where my son is concerned. He does everything his own way. And yet here I am, interfering again.'

'Oh?' She arched an eyebrow in question.

'I have come to ask you to return with me to Cyprus.'

For a moment she stared at him in surprise, but then she shook her head firmly. 'I'm sorry—I can't do that.'

'My son needs you,' he persisted, pleading. 'He is very unhappy.'

'That's his problem,' she countered brutally. 'You said he told you what happened.'

'He told me. And I agree that you were justified in being extremely angry. But, if you once loved him, could you not find it in your heart to forgive him?'

'No. I've already told him that.'

He smiled sadly. 'Ah, you have so much pride. That is good, to have pride—it was the pride in you that made him love you, I think. But take it from me, to throw away love for the sake of pride is a very foolish mistake. I know that, better than most.' His voice had taken on a wistful note. 'Better than most…'

He fell silent, seeming to withdraw into himself. Megan waited, sensing that there was something he wanted to say.

'You know that my wife left me when Theo was still a child? It was because she believed I was having an affair. It wasn't true. Oh, I admit I had an eye for the ladies, but I would never have followed it through. I loved her deeply—from the time I first saw her, she was the only woman I wanted or needed. But I was hurt that she didn't trust me, and so I allowed her to go on thinking the worst—and when she left me I was too proud to beg her to return.' Something sparkled on his cheek—if he had been out in the rain, it could have been a raindrop. 'And then…before I had a chance to come to my senses, and realise how foolishly I was throwing away the best thing in my life…she was killed.'

Megan felt a lump of tears rise in her own throat. 'That's…so sad,' she whispered, covering his thin hand with her own.

He nodded slowly, his eyes intent as they lifted to hers. 'Do not make the same mistake. My son loves you, and you love him. Do not allow my foolishness, and Giorgos's spite, to come between you. Come back with me, and give him another chance.'

She regarded him warily. 'Did he ask you to come?' she queried.

'No. But I think he guessed that I would come to see you while I was in England, and he did not tell me not to.'

'That's not much of a prospect,' she pointed out, a sardonic inflection in her voice.

'He too has his pride. He has been hiding his pain, working very hard. I knew he would be the one to take the business on.'

'So you've got what you wanted.'

The old man shook his head. 'I want him also to be happy. He is my son; I do not want him to endure the long, lonely years without the woman he loves at his side—as I did, through my own stupid pride. He is like me also in that, while his eyes may appreciate many women, his heart will be given only once, irrevocably. Come back with me.'

She drew in a long, slow breath, struggling to resolve the conflicting emotions that were swirling in her brain. 'I'll...think about it,' she conceded at last.

'How long?' he demanded.

'You're rushing me again!'

'That's right. I do not know how long I may have.'

'You really are a wicked schemer, aren't you?'

That wicked grin returned. 'I told you before,' he said merrily, 'I always get my own way.'

It was good to see the sea again—Megan hadn't realised how much she had missed its blue sparkle, the soft whisper of the waves. Slipping off her shoes, she let her toes crunch in the warm sand as she walked down to the water's edge. It was late afternoon, and the sun was setting in a misty haze, painting the sky with streaks of crimson and magenta.

She heard the sound of footsteps crunching over the sand behind her, but she didn't turn her head. She knew it was him. He stopped a few paces behind her, and for a long moment he didn't speak.

'You came back with Papa?'

'Yes.'

'He could persuade you, when I couldn't?' he asked.

'Yes.' There was a harder edge in her voice than she had consciously intended; she was still simmering with anger. 'And you can make of that whatever you like.'

'No.' She heard him sigh—the sigh of a boxer who had taken too many knock-downs and was ready to throw in the towel. 'No, I don't want to make anything of it. I told you I knew I was wrong.' He came closer, until she was aware of the heat of his body inches behind her. 'You've changed your hair.'

'Yes.' She tossed her head, letting the soft breeze from the sea brush the gleaming honey-brown strands across her face. 'That bottle-blonde wasn't really me.'

He laughed, touching his knuckle to the nape of her neck. 'I'd love you whatever colour you wore your hair,' he murmured huskily.

'Would you?' She took a step away from him, and turned—to find herself gazing up into those blue, blue eyes. Funny—she had thought she had forgotten nothing, but she *had* forgotten how incredibly blue they were. And what she saw in them was much too precious to throw away for the sake of mere pride.

'I'm glad you came back.' She saw his throat move with tension, and then abruptly whatever control he had seemed to snap. He reached out for her, dragging her roughly into his arms and almost crushing her in a convulsive embrace, his head buried in the hollow of her shoulder. 'Oh, God, I'm glad you came back.'

She could feel the tears, wet on her cheeks, tears for so many months of bitter loneliness. Why did love have to cause so much pain? She stood on tiptoe, her lips parting hungrily as she sought for his kiss, melting into it as if they had never been apart.

'Don't leave me again,' he growled against her mouth.

'I made so many mistakes, but I love you. Promise me that you'll stay.'

'I'll stay,' she whispered raggedly. 'I'll stay for as long as you want me.'

'As long as that?' His smile was crooked. 'We could be talking about a *very* long time, you know.'

'Sounds good to me,' she responded, her heart soaring with happiness.

He kissed her again, a kiss that was all tenderness— a kiss that told her he had given his heart, irrevocably. The familiar musky scent of his skin was inveigling her senses, making her wonder how she had ever found the strength to walk away from him.

He put his hands against her cheeks, lifting up her face to dust it with kisses. 'I'm sorry I hurt you. You were right—love should be about trust, but I'd never been in love before, and I didn't much like it. I'd always been in control, and suddenly I was totally out of control. It didn't take much for me to convince myself that it had all been a mistake, that I'd been wrong about you. It felt much safer that way.'

She laughed a little unsteadily. 'Maybe that's why I ran away so quickly,' she admitted. 'Why I wouldn't give you a chance to apologise—because it felt safer. Loving you seemed like such a crazy risk to take—there would always have been so many other women trying to sneak in and take my place.'

'What other women?' he asked, his eyes dancing. 'There aren't any other women in the world—only you.'

'You're going to ignore fifty per cent of the world's population?' she queried on a note of dry humour.

'Yes. Well... Okay, so I can't ignore them, not completely,' he acknowledged. 'But there won't ever be a chance that any of them could take your place. You're the only woman I want—now and for ever.'

She smiled up at him, all her love in her eyes. And then, beyond his shoulder, she caught a glimpse of Dakis, standing on the terrace, watching them. 'Your father will be pleased with himself,' she remarked. 'He'll say he knew all along.'

Theo laughed, hugging her close. 'The interfering old goat. Still, he'll be able to have his precious grandson now,' he added, slanting her a meaningful look from eyes that glinted as blue as the warm Mediterranean.

'Or a granddaughter,' she reminded him mischievously.

He shrugged those wide shoulders, scooping her up in his strong arms and tossing her into the air, catching her again as if she weighed nothing at all. 'Grandsons, granddaughters... He can have as many as he likes. I can't think of anything I'd rather do with the rest of my life than spend it making babies with you.'

She wrapped her arms tightly around his neck, resting her cheek against the hard wall of his chest. 'Sounds good to me,' she sighed in blissful contentment.

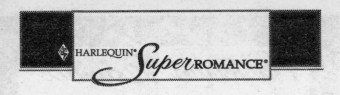

...there's more to the story!

Superromance.

A *big* satisfying read about unforgettable
characters. Each month we offer *six* very different
stories that range from family drama to adventure
and mystery, from highly emotional stories to
romantic comedies—and much more! Stories
about people you'll believe in and care about.
Stories too compelling to put down....

Our authors are among today's *best* romance
writers. You'll find familiar names and talented
newcomers. Many of them are award winners—
and you'll see why!

If you want the biggest and best
in romance fiction, you'll get it
from Superromance!

Emotional, Exciting, Unexpected...

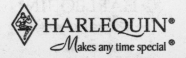

HARLEQUIN®
INTRIGUE

WE'LL LEAVE YOU BREATHLESS!

If you've been looking for thrilling tales of
contemporary passion and sensuous love stories
with taut, edge-of-the-seat suspense—then
you'll love Harlequin Intrigue!

Every month, you'll meet four new heroes
who are guaranteed to make your spine tingle
and your pulse pound. With them you'll enter
into the exciting world of Harlequin Intrigue—
where your life is on the line
and so is your heart!

THAT'S INTRIGUE—
ROMANTIC SUSPENSE
AT ITS BEST!

Makes any time special®

Harlequin® Historical

*From rugged lawmen and
valiant knights to defiant heiresses
and spirited frontierswomen,
Harlequin Historicals will
capture your imagination with
their dramatic scope, passion
and adventure.*

*Harlequin Historicals...
they're too good to miss!*